Recipes and Memoirs
from a
Czech-American Kitchen

by

Augusta Chalabala Wiggs

authorHOUSE®

AuthorHouse™
1663 Liberty Drive, Suite 200
Bloomington, IN 47403
www.authorhouse.com
Phone: 1-800-839-8640

First published by AuthorHouse   11/12/2009

ISBN: 978-1-4343-1419-2 (sc)

Printed in the United States of America
Bloomington, Indiana

This book is printed on acid-free paper.

Introduction
and Special Menus

Always warm the plates so food doesn't congeal while eating.

These recipes and menus are not for the novice

Therefore there are some recipes which are well known to the average cook and need no exact amounts of ingredients or instructions, because these always depend on individual choice.

Only those main dishes, soups, vegetables and desserts which are exceptional or uniqueness in taste, looks are described minutely.

One must <u>like</u> to cook and eat to be a good cook. When being overwhelmed by an acquaintance praise of some specially prepared tidbit, take a good look at the speaker. Does her skin have a good color and tone? Is her complexion glowng (A woman can always tell even when disguised by the latest in make-up creams, etc.). Does she have children? (There must be demands for two or three daily meals so a variety of palates need to be pleased.) When she stands sideways, are there only two things which protrude – her nose and her feet? I have been fooled several times by ecstatic descriptions of something special that turned out to be less than ordinary; a waste of time and money.

When asked for your favorite recipes, I would suggest that you decline by saying it's a secret of your mother's or whatever or tell them it's in this cookbook now on sale, etc. I will tell you why. The recipes you will be asked for are the expensive, intricate ones. Not only is the recipient apt to substitute ingredients and then serve them to you at some future date, but will blame you because the dish did not turn out as expected – never saying a word about substituting chuck for sirloin tip or oleo (ugh!) for butter, etc. And there you are, like a character out of Charles Dickens, somehow or other you have been made to feel guilty because the dinner is not up to expectation.

Clean up after yourself as you go along. Keep a pan of hot soapy water in the sink to take care of used bowls, mixers, odd forks, spoons, pots and pans, etc. So all that needs to be done after dinner are the dishes, glassware, and silverware. Very depressing to come into a kitchen which looks as though a gun had gone off in it.

Be sure to taste whatever you're preparing. Remember you can always add more salt but oversalting will ruin a dish. If you make enough stew, soup, or gravy to have leftovers, use less salt because salt that lays for a day or more becomes saltier.

Always try to use the best ingredients. If you're on a strict budget there are many inexpensive dishes which can be prepared, such as macaroni and cheese with pieces of ham, spaghetti made out of hamburger, as well as chili, tuna and macaroni casseroles, and chicken which is so cheap and can be prepared in many, many delicious ways. If you have toasted cheese sandwiches with vegetable soup and cocoa one night, you can blow yourself to a pound of shrimp and make Shrimp Creole on another night, with rice, waldorf salad and peach cobbler. Or bean soup with a hamhock and corn bread one night, and veal steak or lamb chops another night. All are tasty and healthy, and satisfying.

Our menus revolve around meats, so shop around. I'm sure you know which supermarket carries the best and tenderest beef, the pinkest pork, lamb, or chicken.

Pamper Your Husband!

If he is supporting you, the kids, the dog-cat menagerie, pays all the bills, allows you to be a homemaker instead of a career women and housewife, so draw his bath, lay out his clean clothes, and give him a good breakfast – none of that cold danish and black coffee!

If you don't have a garage, or it's unheated, put an old blanket or coat under the hood of the car to keep it from freezing in the winter. (Of course remove it before starting up.) Tell him what is on the menu for that evening as you kiss him and pat him on his way out the door. Remember he's your true friend. When you sandbagged him in that gorgeous red (or whatever) outfit and had rain drops in your hair, all he wanted was to spend the rest of his life with you. He didn't think about the consequences of saying "I do." I know you didn't either, but I'm sure you had the right perspective on the situation. Anyway, it's better than being the head of a corporation or a liberated woman for life.

If he has a parent or relative who only criticizes and never has a kind word for him, stick up for him and let the jealous one know that you don't want your husband to be criticized and that you think he's wonderful (and count the ways.) Remember he's your true friend.

Shower or bathe before he comes home. If you just can't manage that, keep a toothbrush and toothpaste in the kitchen drawer and use it before he comes home. If he comes home exhausted and irritable, his boss has probably been doing a number on him (knowing that the poor guy has a houseful to support, mortgage payments, etc., etc.) So he's kicked the dog and is yelling a lot. Give him a drink and sit beside him quietly for a few minutes before you serve a tasty and attractive meal.

Keep yourself clean and attractive. Remember he may be working around really gorgeous women. The female is predatory and on the make for a really good man. So wear your spurs and make him glad he married you. Remember practice makes perfect.

A few hints:

Use aluminum cooking utensils, the club type preferably; the aluminum is thick and distributes heat evenly. Any dish which has tomato in it <u>must</u> be prepared in an aluminum or porcelain pan in order to maintain tartness.

Keeping Garlic Fresh: Peel the cloves and place in airtight container. Seal and refrigerate.

How to keep fresh mushrooms: Place on shallow tray or rack. Dip large soft paper towel into cold water. Wring about half dry and lay over mushrooms. Moisten paper toweling each day. Will keep fresh for days this way if stored in the refrigerator on shelf so that cold air will freely pass around the mushrooms. Do not place on bottom of refrigerator or against anything. And do not place mushrooms in waxed paper cups to keep in refrigerator.

How to produce a good fluffiness in a souffle: Use 1/4 t cream of tartar, add it to the beaten egg whites of any standard souffle recipe and bake in the usual slow oven (325). Your souffle will retain its airy poise throughout the meal.

When you seat your guest at dinner, if possible place him/her at a place where there is something attractive to look at or view.

If you have long winters, nothing is as cheerful and uplifts the spirits as a couple of blooming plants – we find the easiest and most colorful are geraniums and african violets. The geraniums have a more interesting foliage, where as violets have a dense, bushy base. I'm sure you know that the violets like minimal sun, but the geraniums flourish in the sun and <u>plenty</u> of water.

Double Duty

In spring, buy pansies, pot them and arrange as a centerpiece. Then into the garden with them.

Freeze whipped cream.

Freeze grapes.

Soak leafy veggies in tepid salt water. All bugs will exit.

Freeze parsley; freeze dill.

Shell and peel chestnuts.

WARM THE PLATES

THE BOSS IS COMING TO DINNER (AND SHE'S A WOMAN)!

(This menu is for the husband's boss, whose wife is allowed to stay home and be a wife and mother. It's a good four hours work.)

Roast Veal
Noodles
Gravy
White Asparagus
Cucumbers in vinegar & oil
Strawberry Bavarian Cream
Sauterne

Ingredients needed:

3-5 lbs. boned shoulder of veal   one large thin cucumber
3-4 strips of meaty bacon   white vinegar
one green pepper   olive oil
2-3 stalks celery   salt & pepper
one large can tomatoes
one large onion
salt & pepper
cream
one lb. wide noodles, wonderful if homemade
one lb can white asparagus

<u>In the morning:</u>
<u>Strawberry Bavarian Cream</u>

Wash and hull berries, sprinkle with sugar and let stand an hour. Then mash and rub berries through a fine sieve. Add the gelatin soaked in cold water and dissolved in boiling water. Chill mixture until it thickens, beat until light, and fold in whipped cream.

Spoon into tall sherbet glasses and allow to chill until dinner time. If you were able to save several perfect berries, place on top of each serving with a mint leaf.

One pint strawberries
½ cup sugar
one pkg (1 tlbs) unflavored gelatin
one cup boiling water
dash salt
One pint whipping cream
(double all ingredients except cream if serving more than four)

<u>Three Hours before Dinner</u>:

<u>Preparation of roast</u>:

Have the butcher bone the veal, and save the bones for stock pot for future aspic. Spread boned veal, salt & pepper it. Now lay the slices of raw bacon horizontally in cavity, as well as the stalks of celery (without green tops) and the sliced green pepper. The meat may not be of even thickness so cut some pieces from thick areas and lay them on the thinner ones. It won't matter because it will be all tied up. Roll the meat and tie with butcher's string at one inch intervals. Place rolled meat in roasting pan, salt & pepper the outside, pour large can of tomatoes over it, and lay sliced onion over all. Cover and bake at 350° for two hours, basting every 30 mins. with juices in pan. When done, remove meat to <u>hot platter</u> and cover with the roasting lid. Make a roux of butter and flour – about 3 tbls to 4 tbls flour – and add sauce from pan and cook until thick. Add chicken broth if too thick. You want about two cups of gravy. Strain gravy and finally add half cup of cream. Gravy will be a beautiful apricot color.

Slice meat into ¾ inch thick slices, between string. Then remove string. Spoon gravy over meat, and pass it at table for noodles which have been buttered and sprinkled with parsley.

Remember to <u>warm dinner plates</u> in the turned off oven

<u>Asparagus</u>: Merely heat, drain and butter.

<u>Cucumbers</u>: Peel, slice and salt them. Drain after 20-30 minutes. Make dressing of one part white white vinegar, three parts water, and one tablespoon sugar. Dissolve and pour over cucumbers and chill. Add one teaspoon olive oil to each serving in individual sauce dishes, just enough to make "eyes" and sprinkle with coarse ground pepper.

Serve the wine throughout the meal.

WARM THE PLATES

IT'S DADDY'S BIRTHDAY! (This is not a dinner for the novice – experience is a must, as in everything.)

Roast Beef & Yorkshire Pudding with gravy
baked potatoes
buttered broccoli
lettuce with Thousand Island dressing
red wine (Burgundy)
Persian nut sundae
coffee

(Nothing tastier or more elegant than a rib roast with Yorkshire pudding and all the rest.)

Buy the first three ribs of a rib roast. These are the best for your money and easiest to carve. Have the chine trimmed to the rib but not removed. If the roast has a long rib, have the butcher saw through the bone but leave it attached. Warn the butcher not to cut into the eye of the roast when he trimming the chine. Show him/her exactly where to cut. The roast will weigh anywhere from six to seven pounds and will serve six generously.

Buy two packages of frozen broccoli.
Get one good red potato for each person.
One large head of lettuce will be adequate.
½ gallon French vanilla ice-cream
Two pints of fudge sauce.
One cup of coarsely chopped pecans.
Have on hand: Lawry's seasoning salt (a must)
    4 eggs
    2 cups milk
    2 cups flour
    salt
    butter
    1 bottle good red wine

Early in the day:

Mix fudge sauce and nuts. Keep at room temperature.

Make large scoops of ice-cream and keep in freezer until ready to serve.

Then heap sauce over ice-cream, covering it completely. (Voila!) Serve the sundae in a large sherbet dish. Be generous with the sauce. You may top it with whipped cream if you wish.

Wash and wipe the meat; salt it generously with Lawry's on all sides, as well as inside the chine cut; heat oven to 325. Roast meat uncovered 25 minutes to the pound for uniform rareness. This means a seven lb. roast will be done in 2 ½ to 3 hours.

Now about the potatoes: The choice between Idahos and red potatoes depends on your preference. Idahos are white and mealy and take to gravy; the red ones are creamy color, moist and have a sweet flavor. They're better with butter. Both should be cut when done and squeezed to force the potato to mound. Then add salt and butter. Potatoes must be scrubbed and rubbed with bacon drippings. Do this by placing a small amount of the drippings in your hand and roll the potatoes in this. The skins will be delicious when done. Place potatoes into a pan the last hour and half of roasting the meat. The extra half hour of roasting is necessary because of the slow oven.

Prepare the Yorkshire pudding while the meat is roasting: After you remove roast and potatoes from oven, set heat up to 450 for the Yorkshire pudding. In the meantime, keep the meat and potatoes as warm as you can without additional cooking. The meat should rest 15 min. anyway, and the pudding is done in 25 mins. It will be ok. Give the guest/s a lovely glass of red wine. (Don't turn on the TV. The commercials at dinner time are rude. Put on a tape of Mozart or Vivaldi.)

While this is baking, cook the frozen broccoli according to directions and add the salt and generous lump of butter.

Yorkshire Pudding:
2 cups milk
2 cups flour
4 eggs
½ tsp. salt

Mix salt & flour and gradually add milk to form a smooth paste. Add eggs and beat two (2)mins. with egg beater. Pour fat off roasting pan to a depth of ¼ inch (into hot lid of the roaster); then pour mixture into hot pan no more than ½ inch deep. Put in hot oven and bake 20 to 30 min. until puffed up and golden brown. Cut in squares for serving. Serve with gravy made from drippings and glaze from roaster. About 3 tbls. fat, 4 tbls flour, made into a roux. Now add the glaze which has been diluted with about two cups cold water or beef broth a little at a time continuously stirring until it thickens. Taste for seasoning. (If gravy is lumpy, put it through a strainer-you can do this, you're alone in the kitchen and, besides, you're in charge).

Mashed potatoes instead of baked potatoes:

Allow one medium potato per serving. 5 boiled potatoes put through a ricer, add 3 Tbls, butter, 1 tsp. salt, few grains pepper, and 1/3 cup HOT milk. Add all ingredients to potatoes, and beat with a fork until creamy, reheat and pile lightly in a <u>hot dish</u>.

Now for serving:

Have salads at each place setting.

<u>Warmed dinner plates</u> at host's left. Unless he's left-handed, then place them at his right. Place roast, from which you have removed the chine, on a <u>warm platter</u> with SHARP carving knife and large fork in front of your hubby. The potatoes, veggies, and pudding are at your end of the table. As he serves the meat and passes it down to you, you serve the accompaniments and serve the guest first if possible. If this is too much trouble, the entire dinner may be served buffet style, with the meat carved into half-inch slices.*

After clearing the table, bring in the dessert and coffee.

*If you have one of those electric warmers for keeping food from congealing, this is a good time to use it for the meat and gravy.

WARM THE PLATES

Lamb Shanks
rice and barley
fried egg plant
Lettuce and grapefruit/Russian drsg
Canned figs/cream

Lamb shanks are expensive considering the small amount of meat on them. However they are delicious. So allow one lamb shank per serving for each lady or child, and two each for the gentlemen.

After washing, place in roaster with cover, salt, garlic powder & pepper, and cover with sliced onions. Add about one cup of water to pan, cover and roast in 350 oven for one and a half hours. Baste every half hour. There should be about one cup of meat juice in the pan. Remove shanks to a covered dish and <u>keep hot</u> without additional cooking.

One cup rice simmered for 25 minutes in 2 cups of salted water.
One half cup washed barley simmered for 40-45 minutes in two cups of water, or until tender. Enough to serve six.
Mix barley and rice into pan drippings and keep hot.

Egg plant:

Peel and cut in thick or thin slices. Sprinkle with salt and pepper. Dredge with flour and saute slowly in butter until crisp and brown. Serve with meat flavored tomato sauce. Leftover spaghetti sauce on this is delicious. (Not good to reheat.)

Chop lettuce and sectioned grapefruit and serve with Russian dressing.

Canned figgs with cream for dessert.

WARM THE PLATES

Caraway Chicken
Noodles
pea pods
banana salad
cherry pudding

Chicken parts – drumsticks, thighs, and breasts. Draw out chicken fat from inside thighs and melt it in a skillet. There should be from one to two tablespoons. Place chicken parts in skillet, salt generously and sprinkle half teaspoon caraway over them. Cover and stew 30 minutes on moderate heat. Now turn pieces over, salt again and again sprinkle caraway. Add about half to full cup water (no more than a cup). Cover and continue to simmer for another half hour. The chicken is done. Remove pieces to <u>hot platter</u> and cover.

Now mix cooked noodles into the lovely juice in the skillet. Be sure noodles are all covered with juice and the chicken fat. If the juice has congealed due to evaporation, add a small amount of hot water, and mix it thoroughly. Sprinkle chopped parsley and mix.

If you can get fresh pea pods you're fortunate. Wash them and destring them if necessary. Now barely cover with hot water, add a little salt, a <u>little</u> sugar, and a piece of butter. Simmer without cover, stirring all the time, for not more than five minutes.

The banana salad is kid stuff but no adult has ever refused it. Mask skinned banana in mayonnalse or miracle whip and sprinkle generously with crushed salted peanuts. Lay on chopped lettuce; funny but tasty.

Cherry Pudding – Put 6 T flour into a mixing bowl with a pinch of salt. Stir in 3 eggs, one at a time & gradually add 3 cups milk and 4 T sugar. Arrange a layer of unpitted black sweet cherries in the bottom of a buttered 9" cake pan. Pour the liquid mixture over the cherries and bake in a slow oven 300 for 30 min or until it is firm. Sprinkle with sugar while it is still hot. <u>Serve warm</u>.

WARM THE PLATES

BLACK-EYED PEAS AND HAMHOCKS

Black-eyed peas & hamhocks
Rye bread & butter
Beer & peeled tomatoes
Wilted lettuce & sliced tomatoes
Baked apples
Choc chip cookies

Ingredients:
2 cups blackeye peas
2 or 3 ham hocks
1 large onion
1 large potato
1 stalk celery
Head lettuce
Vinegar & sugar
2-3 T olive oil
One large apple per serving

Soak blackeyed peas overnite. Drain, cover/water. Wash hamhocks. Add about 6-8 cups cold water. Slice onion and celery and add to peas and hamhocks. Simmer for two hours. Cube potato and add to above and continue cooking slowly for another 30 to 40 minutes. Remove hamhocks; strip meat and skin off bones and cut all in bite size pieces. If you don't like the skin, mix it into your dog's food. (he'll love you for it). However, remember that the skin adds a different texture, is tasty and because it's gelatinous, it's good for your nails and hair (I swear).

Serve the above in large soup bowls with buttered rye bread on the side. The ryr b & b is a must or you will have to carry a lighted candle.

Tear lettuce into medium pieces. Mix 1/3 cup white vinegar to 2/3 cups water. Dissolve one tablespoon sugar in it and add olive oil. Pour mix over letttuce early in the afternoon and refrigerate. The lettuce will be limp by suppertime. Stir it a couple of times during the afternoon so all pieces are coated with dressing. Peeled, sliced and lightly salted tomatoes on the side.

Roman apples are best for baking because they're large and meaty. However, any apples will do. Wash, core and peel sour apples. (sprinkle lemon juice over the apples to enhance flavor) Put in a baking dish and fill cavities with sugar & spice. Allow ½ c sugar and ½ t cinnamon or nutmeg to 8 apples. Cover bottom of the dish with boiling water & bake in hot oven 400 F until soft, basting often with syrup in dish. Serve <u>hot</u> or cold with cream.

Choc chip cookies
Serves six to 8 generously

1 C & 2 T flour
½ t baking soda
½ t salt
½ c softened butter
6 T sugar
6 T finely packed brn sugar
½ t vanilla
1 egg
1 6 oz pkg semi sweet choc chips
½ c chopd nuts

Preheat oven 375

In small bowl combine flour, soda, salt & set aside. In large bowl combine butter, sugar, brown sugar & vanilla, beat until creamy. Beat in egg. Gradually add flour mixture. Stir in choc chips & nuts. Drop by level measuring T onto greased cookie sheet. Bake 9-11 min. Makes about 2 ½ doz 2 1/4" cookies.

WARM THE PLATES

**Smoked picnic
Kentucky wonders cooked with pork skin
baked yams
cukes in vinegar
pineapple turnovers**

Smoked picnic used to be very inexpensive; now even at 1.39 cents perlb., when bones, skin, and fat are removed, the cost of the meat is more than two dollars per pound. However, it has its advantages. First wash the joint, then remove the skin. Cut the skin into one inch strips and cook them along with the kentucky wonder beans. The flavor is excellent, and the skin is tender and tasty. Trim off asmuch of the fat as possible. Cut it into cubes and render it over a low fire. Pour off the rendered fat and save it for frying. It should be almost white when congealed. Put the cracklings through a ricer, and voila! Break up the cracklings and serve them to your hubby with a bottle of beer. He'll love you for it.

Bake the picnic for about 1½-2 hrs at 320-350 along with scrubbed yams, one per serving.

wash the beans.

String the beans; ½ # break them into two inch pieces and set them to cook with the ham skins in enough water to cover. Cook them gently for a good hour. They should be cooked thoroughly, not like snap beans.

Two Sliced, salted, and drained cukes. Cover them with 1 part vinegar to 3 parts water, plus 1 T sugar. Chill them. Add one or two tablespoons of olive oil and several gratings of pepper before serving. Serve them individually in sauce dishes.

Pineapple turnovers Make your own pastry squares, (same as pie dough). Make squares about 4 inches square. Place one T of pineapple preserves in center of each square. Brush edges with water; fold the dough into triangles and press edges to seal. Pierce tops Brush tops with milk or egg yolk diluted with a little water. Bake about 15 min. in hot oven 425-450. If this is too much trouble, I suggest two cartons of crescent rolls, each of which contains eight triangles. This will make only four turnovers. Make eight - they won't go to waste.

About the bones - If your dog is not allowed to have bones, throw away the small bones and give the big one to your neighbor's dog. It's always nice to be on friendly terms with a watchdog.

Serves 4 to 8

Recipes and Memoirs from a Czech-American Kitchen

WARM THE PLATES

Irish Stew with Dumplings
Sliced tomatoes
Pumpkin Pie
Coffee

Ingredients:
3 lbs boned lamb shoulder cut in chunks
½ cup carrots cubed
½ cup turnip cubed
¼ cup barley
one sliced onion
4 cups sliced potstoes
¼ cup flour
salt & pepper
Dumplings

Have kettle with boiling water, enough to more than cover the meat. Put meat into boiling water and cook slowly one hour. Then add the salt, carrots, turnip, onion and barley (which has been washed). After another 30 minutes add the sliced potatoes. If necessary, thicken with flour with ¼ cup cold water. This may not be necessary due to the thickening agents of the barley and potatoes. Again, remember this is a stew and there must be a thick liquid covering the meat.

Now add the dumplings:
2 cups flour
3 t baking powder
¾ cup milk
½ t salt

Mix and sift dry ingredients. Add milk gradually. Toss on floured board, pat and roll out half an inch thick. Shape with biscuit cutter, dipped in flour. Place biscuits on top of stew, Cook 12 minutes, closely covered.

Peeled, sliced lightly salted tomatoes are refreshing with this.

Pumpkin pie:
Unbaked pastry shell. Fill with
2 eggs slightly beaten
one can 16 oz. solid pack pumpkin
¾ cup brown sugar
½ t salt
¼ t ground cloves
1 t ground cinnamon

½ t ground ginger
1-13 oz. can evaporated milk
whipped cream for topping

Preheat overn to 425°. Mix filling ingredients in order given. Pour into pie shell. Bake 15 minutes. Reduce heat to 350° and continue baking 45 minutes or until knife inserted near center of pie comes out clean. Cool completely on wire rack. Serve with whipped cream.

WARM THE PLATES

CHICKEN & RICE
Peas
Shredded lettuce & tomato salad
custard with maple syrup

In greased pen (pyrex) put two cups uncooked rice. Lay two cut up chickens skin side up on top of rice. Mix together one cup cream of mushroom soup and two cups orange juice (no kidding!) Pour mixture over chicken & rice. Sprinkle one envelope Lipton's onion soup mix over top. Cover with foil and bake two hours at 325°.

2 pkgs Frozen peas, cook according to directions but add 2 T of butter.

Custard:
4 cups scalded milk,
4 to 6 eggs depending on size
½ cup sugar
¼ t salt, few gratings nutmeg

Beat eggs slightly, add sugar & salt. Pour on slowly scalded milk and pour into buttered mold. Set in pan of hot water, sprinkle with nutmeg & bake in moderate oven (350) until firm, about 35 min. To test, insert knife in custard, if knife comes out clean, custard is done. Don't let water surrounding custard come to a boil while baking or custard will whey. For cup custards allow four eggs to 4 cups milk; for large molded custard, six eggs. Replace 1 T milk by 1 T evaporated milk to make custard cut perfectly. This last is really optional, and not necessary. Serve with maple syrup, or diluted blueberry jam.

Nice for a ladies' luncheon. or family supper

Serves 8

WARM THE PLATES

Roast Chicken with stuffing
green asparagus
dilled new potatoes
Apricot Charlotte Russe
Bib Lettuce
Italian drsg

one 4lb. chicken (not a hen) Rinse, dry, and s & p inside. Remove giblets and cook them in two cups of water with one onion & stalk of celery. Salt to taste.

Stuff with the following: 4 cups bread cubes, 1 c celery
1 t salt
1 t thyme
½ t pepper
1/3 cup melted butter
½ cup chicken broth

Use stale bread and cut in ½ inch cubes. Add seasonings, mix well. Add melted butter & stock. Spoon into chicken cavity and sew up. Rub chicken with butter, season it with salt and pepper add 1 c water and roast in 350 oven for 1 ½ to two hrs. basting frequently with fat and juices in pan. Add water as needed.

Boil small red potatoes in their jackets. Allow two per serving. They will be done in about 25 minutes. Peel while hot and pour freshly made dill sauce over them. Set them aside for about 30 min. Dill sauce: To one or two cups of white sauce add vinegar to taste and boil. add fresh dill minced fine and several tablespoons of sour cream. Reheat them before serving but do not boil.

Apricot Charlotte Russes: l large pkg apricot gelatin
½ c sugar
2 c boiling water
1 T lemon juice
1½ c apricot nectar
2 c whipped cream
1 pkg lady fingers, split

Dissolve gelatin & sugar in boiling water. Add lemon juice & nectar. Chill until slightly thickened, fold in whipped cream. Line sides of 9 inch oiled spring form pan with lady fingers and fill with gelatin mixture. Chill until very firm; remove sides of pan and garnish with canned, drained apricot halves if desired. If you use large can of canned apricots you may use the syrup in place of nectar.

Bib lettuce

Green Asparagus:

Soak fresh asparagus in several cold waters to release all sand/soil. Trim off any tough ends. Cut stems in half. Cover bottoms with cold salted water and cook quickly for 10 min. Then add tops of asparagus which are more tender, and simmer them for another ten to fifteen minutes. (Don't drown them.) When done, pour melted butter over all and serve <u>hot</u>.

Menus Featuring Fish

Luncheon Clambake, Salad, Spinach, Biscuits, Peaches and Cream

Luncheon Clambake, salad, cut up tomato, celery, apple, radish on lettuce leaf, marinated with French dressing, buttered spinach, biscuits, and peaches and cream. Coffee or tea.

Clambake:

4 eggs
4 cups milk
2-1/2 cups soda cracker crumbs (about 30 crackers)
1/3 cup melted butter
2 cans chopped clams with liquid
2 T minced green pepper
½ t salt, dash pepper
½ t Wooster sauce (you know)
2 cut up crab legs
2 thinly sliced green onions

Beat eggs well; add milk, cracker crumbs, and let stand 20 minutes. Add butter, rest of ingredients. Taste, add more salt if needed. Pour into greased 8 x 8" pan. Refrigerate for at least an hour.

One hour before serving: bake one hour at 350 or 325 (in glass). Cut into squares and serve with anchovy sauce. White sauce (omit salt and pepper). Add ¾ to one teaspoon anchovy paste and two tablespoons minced celery.

Salad: As stated above.

Spinach: One or two packages frozen spinach leaves. Allow to thaw and cut off stems. Examine thoroughly for little critters. We all make mistakes. Cook according to directions; use chicken broth instead of water. Taste for seasoning. Add a quartered hard boiled egg on each serving.

Biscuits: Buy the good brand of store-bought frozen biscuits. Cut them in half, so they look like crescents, lay them in buttered pan, brush them with melted butter and a small sprinkling of sugar. *Yummy!* Be sure to lay them in clean napkin in the server and cover them with the napkin. (They dry out if left uncovered.)

Peaches and Cream:

6-8 ripe peaches. Boil a quart of water; immerse preaches two at a time, count to 20, remove them and the skins should slide off. It may take longer – it's no big deal to put them back in the water for a couple of seconds.

Now slice them and sugar them generously. Refrigerate in a covered container. Serve in fruit dishes with the cream. *(Now stand back – your guests may want to embrace you.)*

Serves 8

Crab stuffed Fillet of Sole, Spring Salad, Tin Roof Sundae, Iced Tea

Ingredients:
4 fillets of sole, about 2 lbs.
1 med. white onion minced
2 T butter

1 can crab meat (6 to 7 oz.) or six imitation crab legs now available in the fish departments of most supermarkets. If you use these cut them into half-inch pieces.

1 four-oz. can mushrooms, drained and chopped

½ cup coarse cracker crumbs, about 6-8 sprigs parsley, minced

1 cup shredded Swiss cheese

Make sauce of 3 T butter, 3 T flour, salt, 1 ½ cups milk and one cup (4 oz.) shredded Swiss cheese

Lay fillets white side down in buttered Pyrex dish, sprinkle with salt and pepper. Set aside while you make the stuffing. Combine the onion and butter and cook until tender. Do not brown. Stir in the crab meat, mushrooms and cracker crumbs. Season well with salt and pepper. Divide stuffing evenly, spread almost the full length of each fillet. Sandwich stuffing between 2 fillets. Pour sauce over all and cook for 35-40 mins. in 325 degree oven.

Salad:
½ cup cooked asparagus   ½ t salt
½ cup cooked string beans   ½ t mustard
½ cup cooked peas   2 T vinegar

½ cup sliced radishes	6 T olive oil
2 artichoke bottoms, cooked and sliced	¼ cup mayonnaise
2 hard cooked chopped eggs	dash of pepper

Mix together salt, pepper, dry mustard, vinegar and olive oil in a salad bowl. Add vegetables, toss all together, and let marinate ½ to 1 hour. Just before serving add mayonnaise.

Tin Roof Sundae:

Are you old enough to remember these? Chocolate ice cream covered with marshmallow cream with a generous sprinkling of chopped nuts. *Pass that whipped cream!*

Serve 5-6

Orange Roughie, Green Beans, Green Salad, Lemon Tarts.

Orange Roughie with cream of shrimp soup, rice, green beans, salad and lemon cream tarts

Ingredients:
2 lbs fish
1 can cream of shrimp soup

Butter pyrex dish, lay fillets of fish in dish and cover with the shrimp soup which has been diluted with ¼ - ½ cup milk. Bake in 325 oven for 30-40 minutes. Sprinkle with chopped parsley and serve with hot cooked rice and the boiled, buttered green beans.

Any kind of green salad goes well with this.

Now for the tarts:

Invert a pan of muffin tins. Press a circle of pastry dough over each tin. Pierce with a fork and bake in 450 degree oven for about 10 minutes. Watch it. When cool, remove tarts and fill each with lemon cream, cover with meringue.

Lemon filling:

1 ½ cups sugar	4 egg yolks
2 cups boiling water	lemon rind 1 T freshly grated or ½ T dry
5 T cornstarch	6 T lemon juice
5 T flour	2 T butter

Mix cornstarch, flour and sugar and add boiling water, stirring constantly. Stir until mixture boils, then cook 20 minutes in double boiler. Add butter, egg yolks, rind and the lemon juice. When cool, fill the tarts, leaving room for the meringue.

Note: If you're not a purist, we have found the Jello lemon pie filling very satisfactory – and a lot less work.

Scalloped Oysters, Creamed Vegetables, Carrot and Raisin Salad, Plum Dumplings

Ingredients needed:

1 pint oysters	1 pkg frozen mixed vegetables
½ cup bread crumbs	3-4 grated carrots
1 cup cracker crumbs	handful white raisins
½ cup melted butter	French dressing salt and pepper
Cream – 2 T	6 Italian plums stoned
Oyster liquor – 4 T	Four medium size potatoes cooked and mashed
	1 cup flour
	cinnamon and sugar and butter

<u>Method of Preparation:</u>

Mix bread and cracker crumbs and salt and pepper. Put a thin layer in bottom of shallow, buttered baking dish. Cover with oysters and sprinkle with salt and pepper. Add half each oyster liquor and cream. Repeat and cover top with remaining crumbs. Bake 30 minutes in hot oven at 435 degrees. (Never allow more then two layers of oysters for scalloped oysters.)

Golf ball size of dough - insert plum pinch shut. Place in boiling salted H20. Add flour make dough 6 min. boil it each side. Then, put in a bowl, "open it" and sprinkle cinnamon/ sugar butter.

Cook frozen mixed vegetables as directed. When cooked, add one tablespoon of flour; mix thoroughly into vegetables, then add ½ to 1 cup milk, depending on how thick you want the cream sauce. Finally blend in one tablespoon butter and cook until thickened over low heat.

Carrot and Raisin Salad: Grate four medium peeled carrots. Add ½ white raisins, and mask with French dressing.

This is a good early fall dinner. The dumplings are "ethnic" – different and interesting.

Serves 4 generously.

Fish Dinner Menu
Clam Chowder
Shrimp Creole with Rice
Lettuce, avocado and grapefruit salad
Strawberry shortcake and coffee

Ingredients needed:

Soup
8 oz. can chopped clams
1 ½ inch cube salt pork
1 sliced onion
2 medium potatoes
2 T butter
2 cups scalded milk or half and half

Shrimp Creole: prepare in aluminum pan
¼ cup butter
1 large can tomatoes
1 medium onion
half green pepper
2 stalks celery
1 clove garlic, one bay leaf salt and pepper
one T chili powder
one t sugar, salt and pepper to taste
1 lb. green shrimp (uncooked)
two cups cooked rice

Salad
1 avocado
grapefruit
Lettuce
French dressing

Shortcake
two packages biscuits from dairy case one
one quart berries lettuce
pint whipping cream

This is a fairly light supper so a bowl of hot clam chowder is just right.

Clam Chowder: Wash salt pork, cut in small pieces and try out in butter; add sliced onion and fry five minutes. Add cut up potatoes, two cups boiling water and cook until potatoes are done and have thickened the soup. Now add drained clams, hot cream and season to taste. Heat clam water and thicken with one T butter and flour cooked together. Add to chowder just before serving. Serves 4.

Shrimp Creole: Chop onion, pepper, celery and fry until limp in ¼ cup butter; add tomatoes and other seasonings and cook 30 to 40 minutes before adding shrimp (which have been peeled and deveined.) Continue cooking until shrimps are tender, about 8-10 minutes or until shrimp are pink but not tightly curled. Add a little flour to sauce to thicken. Remove bay leaf and garlic. Make a ring of cooked rice and pour the shrimp into the center.

<u>Salad:</u> Peel grapefruit, break into segments, and using a fairly sharp knife, cut membrane down center of segment and peel off. Peel avocado, slice into thin slices, sprinkle with lemon (to prevent turning black) and lay alternate pieces of grapefruit and avocado in a circle on torn pieces of lettuce. Drizzle with French dressing.

(This is a very sophisticated menu.)

Shrimps a la Newburg, Stuffed tomato salad,
Banana bread spread with cream cheese, coffee or tea

Shrimp a la Newburg

1 lb. shrimps	1 t lemon juice
3 T butter	few grains cayenne pepper
½ t salt	1 T flour
yolks 2 eggs	½ cup cream
	2 T Sherry

Serve a glass of chilled sauterne (we like the Taylor wines)

Clean shrimps and cook in two T butter three minutes. Add salt, cayenne, lemon juice, and cook one minute. Remove shrimps, and put remaining butter into pan. Add flour and cream. When thickened, add slightly beaten yolks, shrimps and wine. Serve in pastry shells. Buy them. (in the freezer section of your market.)

Stuffed Tomato Salad – Peel 4 medium sized tomatoes. Remove thin slice from top of each and take out seeds and some of the pulp. Sprinkle inside with salt; invert and let stand one half hour. Fill tomatoes with cucumbers (remove seeds) cut in small cubes and celery and mix with mayonnaise. Arrange on lettuce leaves.

Banana Bread:

½ cup butter	2 eggs
1 ½ t baking powder	½ t baking soda; ¼ t salt
¼ cup sour cream	1 cup sugar
2 cups flour	1 cup mashed bananas (2 large or 3 sm)
2 T milk	1 T almond extract
	1 ½ cups chopped pecans

Do this in the morning so bread will slice easily.

Cream butter and sugar, beat in eggs and sour cream. Sift flour, baking powder, baking soda and salt. Blend into creamed mixture alternately with mashed bananas. Add milk and flavoring, stir in pecans. Turn into greased 9 by 3 inch loaf pan. Bake at 350 for 60-70 minutes. Remove bread from pan and cool. Moisten cream cheese with cream, mash, and spread between thin slices of banana bread.

Serves 4

Tuna casserole
Grapefruit and celery salad
Chocolate sundae

2 small cans tuna in water or oil
7 oz sea shells or macaroni (sea shells are prettier)
1 can cream of mushroom soup
1 can button mushrooms
1 medium onion fried in butter
almonds

Precook macaroni in boiling water for five minutes. Fry onion to limp stage, and add soup plus one can of water. Drain tuna and break it up with fork in soup/onion mixture, mixing thoroughly, but don't mash the tuna. Finally add mushrooms with liquid.

Add slivered almonds which have been lightly toasted in butter. Sprinkle these over the tuna casserole just before serving.

Butter an oblong pyrex pan, mix macaroni and tuna lightly, spread it in the pan and bake in 325 oven for 30 minutes.

Grapefruit and celery salad:
2-3 grape fruit
2-4 stalks celery
honey/french dressing

Cut grapefruit in half, remove pulp and add equal quantity of finely cut celery. Mask with French dressing sweetened with a bit of honey. Serve on shredded lettuce.

Yield 4-6 portions

Salmon Loaf with clam chowder, mashed potatoes, baby limas, tomato aspic, crepes with strawberry jam

Salmon Loaf – 2 cups flaked salmon
1 cup fine bread crumbs
½ stick butter melted
½ cup hot milk

3 eggs slightly beaten
2 T minced parsley
salt and pepper

Combine ingredients in order given. Press into buttered bread pan. Bake 30-40 minutes in moderate oven 350.

Clam chowder without the potatoes, heated and served as gravy with loaf. Or you may use half diluted cream of shrimp soup.

Mashed potatoes, allow one medium potato per serving.

Frozen lima beans prepared according to directions, adding T of butter.

Tomato Aspic: We use 1 T unflavored gelatin dissolved in bit of cold water. Add this to a small can of tomato juice with finely cut celery and onion, and radish. Pour back into can and allow to jell. For serving, cut into 1 ½ inch rounds, top with bit of creamed mayonnaise and parsley.

Serve aspic in lettuce cups.

Crepes with strawberry jam:
1 cup flour
2/3 cup milk
2/3 cup water

3 eggs, salt
3 T melted butter

Beat all with wire whisk, allow to rest 15 minutes at least.

Fry each crepe in 1 T butter (just like panacakes.) Remove to platter, spread with homemade strawberry jam and roll up. Sprinkle with sifted powdered sugar.

Serves 4-6

**Ladies bridge luncheon – a glass of white wine or Sherry for an appetizer
Scallops, Lyonnaise potatoes, cucumber and tomato salad,
hot biscuits with honey in the comb, iced tea**

1 lb. scallops, salt and pepper, rolled in flour, dipped in beaten egg, and coated with cracker meal. Fry in bacon drippings. Drain on paper towels and keep warm.

Potatoes: 4 T butter, one small onion thinly sliced and fried in butter for about 5 minutes. Add three cups cold boiled potatoes, sliced, sprinkle with salt and pepper and stir until well mixed. Cover and cook slowly until potato is brown underneath, fold, and turn on hot platter. Sprinkle with finely chopped parsely.

About cucumbers: always peel, slice or dice the cucumber, add salt and set aside for 20 minutes. Pour off the accumulated water and then add to tomato or other salad fixings. No one will complain about indigestion from eating cucumbers if the cuke is first marinated and drained.

If you serve biscuits with butter and fresh honey in the comb, no dessert will be needed.

Iced tea: Strain hot tea into glasses ½ full of cracked ice. Garnish with slices of lemon, plus small pitchers of simple syrup for sweetening and more sliced lemon. Quick chilling results in a clear tea with a fine flavor.

The entire luncheon can be served on one plate; pass the biscuits in an attractive basket with a white linen napkin. Serve the honey in the comb, allowing each guest to help herself.

Serves 4

Ladies Luncheon
A glass of sauterne before lunch
Creamed salmon with peas
Bib lettuce with diced grapefruit, green pepper, orange, sliced radish, masked
with French dressing to which a bit of lime juice and honey has been added.
Caramelized biscuits, coffee

1 Large can red salmon, drained, backbone and skin removed. Break into chunks and heat in two cups of cream sauce.

4 T butter	2 cups milk or half and half
4 T flour	½ t salt and bit of white pepper (watch this-it's very strong)

Melt butter, add flour mixed with seasoning, and stir until well blended. Pour on milk/cream gradually while stirring constantly. Bring to boiling point and boil for two minutes. (If the sauce has lumps, strain it into another pan. *The sauce won't have lumps if you prepare it in a double boiler!*) Add the salmon and bring it up to heat. Then just before serving, add the frozen, cooked peas. Do not let the peas sit in the salmon/sauce mix or it will sweeten the sauce. *Ugh!*

Salad: Bib lettuce is pretty and tasty. Peel outer and inner skins of oranges and grapefruit, cut in bite size pieces along with sliced radishes and green peppers and pour a small amount of dressing over all.

Caramelized Biscuits:

2 cups unbleached flour	3 T lard
4 t baking powder	¾ to 1 cup milk or half milk & half water
1 t salt	

Mix dry ingredients and sift once. Work in shortening with pastry blender. Add liquid gradually, mixing with fork to soft dough. Easy with the liquid – differences in flour. Toss on floured board, pat, and roll LIGHTLY ½ inch thick. Shape with small biscuit cutter. Melt 4 T butter in round cake pan, cover with ½ cup brown sugar. Place biscuits on top of butter/sugar mixture and bake 15 minutes in hot oven 450. When done, place warm chop plate over cake pan and invert onto chop plate. Allow this to sit for a time to allow syrup to melt over biscuits. Serve at once. Serves 4

**Baked Stuffed Fish, Stewed tomatoes, Pineapple and cottage cheese on lettuce,
French Drop Doughnuts, Boiled riced potatoes**

One whole whitefish about 3 lbs. or fillets of sole

5 T butter	¼ cup chopped parsley
3 T chopped celery	1 cup light cream
1 T chopped sweet onion	1 T flour
1 cup bread crumbs	½ cup white wine

½ lb. crab meat, flaked (or fake crabs legs)

Melt 4 T of butter and sauté onion and celery until onion is limp. Add crab meat salt and pepper, bread crumbs, parsley, and ¼ cup of cream and mix well. Stuff the fish loosely with mixture, or layer it between fillets of sole. Make sauce out of remaining butter, cream, flour and wine. Pour over fish and bake at 320 for 35-45 minutes in pyrex dish.

Stewed tomatoes: Del Monte stewed tomatoes are excellent. Add 1 T butter and a slice of cubed buttered toast and heat.

Riced Potatoes

Lettuce, ring of canned pineapple topped with small curd cottage cheese. Some prefer the cottage cheese with a dab of honey. We like ours plain.

French Drop Doughnuts

1 cup water	¼ cup butter
3 T sugar	1/8 t salt
1 t grated orange rind	1 cup flour
3 eggs	

Place water, sugar, rind, butter and salt in a saucepan and bring to boil. Add flour all at once and cook for a minute or two, stirring constantly until mixtures leaves sides of pan. Turn into bowl and cool slightly. Add eggs, one at a time and beat until mixture is smooth. You way use a rotary beater or electric mixer. Drop from a teaspoon into hot fat (lard) at 365 degrees. Balls will brown and then crack. Turn and brown on all sides, 3 to 4 minutes in all. Drain on paper towels. Cool and roll in sugar. These little doughnuts are unbelievably light and melt-in-the-mouth. Eat while warm. Do not reheat. If it's for the family, serve them with ice cold milk.

Serves 4-6

Fried Haddock, Potato pancakes, creamed corn, cole slaw, baked apples with cream, and tapioca

Defrost frozen haddock, or use fresh skinned haddock fillets. If frozen ones are too wet, dry them somewhat with paper towels. Now cut fish into inch chunks, salt and pepper them and roll them in flour, then in beaten egg and finally in cracker and bread crumbs. (That's right; just like fried chicken)

Melt bacon drippings in skillet so fat half-covers the fish chunks. Fry uncovered over medium heat and keep an eye on them. Fish cook very quickly. As with other fried foods, when tops of fish show juices, turn them over gently and fry other side. A whole skillet-full will be done in 20 to 25 minutes.

Potato Pancakes; Grate 3 medium sized raw potatoes, one tablespoon flour, 1 tablespoon cream, 1 egg and 1 t salt. Mix all ingredients. Stir well, cook by spoonfuls in heavy frying pan in hot fat. Do these while you're frying the fish. Don't dawdle or the raw potatoes will darken. It won't spoil them, but they won't look nice. Use lard.

Use the best grade of canned cream corn, white preferred, and add a can of regular corn, shoepeg if you can get it, to the cream. Add 1 T butter, heat and serve.

Baked apples: Tapioca: 2 ½ cups boiling water
1/8 t salt
6 sour apples
½ cup sugar
½ cup quick-cooking tapioca

Add tapioca to boiling water and salt; cook in double boiler until transparent. Core and pare half way down apples, arrange in buttered dish, fill cavities with sugar, pour over tapioca and bake in 350 oven until apples are soft. Serve with cream. If the apples aren't sour enough add a quarter teaspoon of lemon juice to sugar for each apple.

Cole Slaw: You will use such a small amount of this that it will pay you to buy a pint at the local deli. However, if you are a purist, here's how: Shred cabbage and soak in cold water until crisp; drain, dry between paper towels and mix with this dressing:

¼ t salt	2 T butter
1 t mustard	¾ cup milk
2/3 t sugar	¼ cup vinegar
one egg, slightly beaten	

Mix dry ingredients, add egg, butter, milk and vinegar very slowly. Stir and cook over boiling water until mixture begins to thicken. Cool. Serve.

Asian Supper

**Anchovy dressing served over tossed greens, cherry tomatoes, green pepper chunks
Meringue shells with ice cream and crushed sweetened
pineapple (canned) poured over ice cream
or
Pound cake sandwiches with butter pecan ice
cream. Freeze; serve with chocolate sauce**

Shrimp Egg Foo Young

6 eggs slightly beaten	3 T lard or bacon drippings
1 can (4 ½ oz) shrimp or one cup cooked shrimp	½ or 8 oz. can bean sprouts
½ cup chopped onion	drained and rinsed.
¼ t salt and dash of pepper	

Cook onion in one T hot lard until tender but not brown. Combine slightly beaten eggs, shrimp, bean sprouts, onions, salt and pepper. Cook egg mixture slowly (like pancakes) in remaining hot shortening in skillet. Run spatula under edge. Turn egg foo young to cook other side. Serve with brown sauce.

Brown sauce: 1 T butter, 2 t cornstarch, 1 t sugar, 1- ½ T soy sauce. Melt butter, combine cornstarch with sugar and blend into butter. Add ½ c bean sprout juice (or water) and soy sauce. Cook, stirring constantly until mixture is thick and bubbly. Makes ¾ cup.

Chow Mein

½ lb. pork cut in thin strips	3 cups thin bias-cut celery
½ lb. beef cut in thin strips	1 cup sliced onion (one medium)
3 T lard	1 can of best mushrooms sliced and drained
1 – ½ cup beef broth (homemade)	1 can (16 oz) chow mein veggies, drained
¼ cup soy sauce	3 T cornstarch – ¼ cup cold water

Cook pork and beef in 1 T lard about 10 minutes. Add beef broth and ¼ c soy sauce. Simmer while cooking vegetables about 15 minutes. Cook celery, onions and mushrooms in 2 T lard until crisp but tender, stirring often. Combine with the cooked meat. Blend cornstarch and cold water together. Add to the meat and veggies, stirring until thick. Add chow mein veggies. Serve over rice or chow mein noodles.

Fried eggplant

Sift I cup flour and ½ t salt. Add two eggs and about ¾ cups milk to make a medium thin batter. Cut one medium unpeeled eggplant into ¼" slices and dip them in the batter. Fry same in ½" corn oil in heavy skillet until golden brown on both sides. Turn slices only once. Drain eggplant on paper towels, and sprinkle with grated Romano cheese or serve them with tomato sauce (left over spaghetti sauce only) The spaghetti sauce is the better of the two. Eat while hot. Do not reheat. Some foods are better the second day; this is not one of them.

Creole Halibut Steak, Pear & Spinach salad, German Apple Pancake

2 halibut steaks (about 1 ½ lb. each)
Salt and pepper
1 cups soft bread crumbs
1 T minced parsley
3 T melted butter
2 T lemon juice
1 ½ t granted lemon rind
1 can condensed Manhattan clam chowder

Have steaks cut about ½ inch thick. Place one in bottom of buttered baking dish. Sprinkle with salt and pepper and spread with a dressing made with all ingredients, except the chowder. Cover with remaining steak. Pour the clam chowder over all. Bake in moderate over 350 about one hour until done. Serve immediately. *Delicious.*

Pear and Spinach salad: Core, peel and slice thinly two fresh winter pears. Combine pear slices with half pound washed and torn spinach, ½ cup croutons, one peeled and sliced avocado. Toss with vinegar and oil dressing. Add avocado and pear just before tossing with dressing so they don't turn grey.

German Apple Pancake

Blend 3 eggs, ½ c milk, 1/3 c flour and ¼ t salt until smooth. Let the batter stand covered for one hour. Core, Peel and halve two medium green apples and slice them thinly. Put the slices in a bowl and sprinkle them with 2 T lemon juice. In a heavy 11" skillet heat 3 T butter and pour in batter. Cover it with apple slices and bake the pancake in 375 oven for 10-15 minutes until it is puffy and set. Slide the pancake onto a dish and spread it with 2 T well softened butter and sprinkle it with ¼ cup sugar with ¼ t cinnamon. Serves 4 to 6.

Hearty Winter Menus

Buffet Supper
(Time approximately 3 hours)
Baked ham (precooked) butt end 5-6 lbs.
Baked yams (one for each serving)
Green beans (1- ½ lbs. fresh or 2 pkgs frozen)
Fried Apples (3 to 4 apples cored and sliced in half-inch slices)
Rolls and Biscuits
Blueberry or Strawberry Shortcake
Salad – celery hearts, carrot sticks, olives, etc.
Coffee

Skin ham (save skin), cut off most of fat (save this for making ham drippings and cracklings – more about this later.) Score the ham and rub with one cup brown sugar, two T vinegar and one T mustard, mixed. Insert one clove in each diamond. Place fat side up in uncovered pan at 325 for two hours This is enough time for about half a ham. An entire precooked ham should be baked longer.

Scrub yams and bake at same time as ham – allowing 1 – ½ to 2 hours at 325.

Bake biscuits in the morning and keep them covered so they don't dry out

Cook beans according to directions and add 2 tablespoons butter.

Core apples and slice them. Omit ends. Sprinkle with sugar and fry them in butter, turning once until soft; add drop of lemon juice if apples are not tart.

For dessert use two biscuits for each serving of shortcake. Add about half cup water to jar of blueberry or strawberry preserves and heat if fresh fruit is not available. For fresh fruit mash half with sugar and add whole berries to remainder. Spoon berries over biscuits and top with whipped cream.

Proceed as follows:
1. WARM THE PLATES slice ham in kitchen and place on sideboard. Cut yams in half and score them, adding salt and butter to each.
2. Warm rolls in oven after removing ham and yams. Put rolls into serving dish on white napkin and cover to keep warm.
3. Put beans into hot covered vegetable dish and apples on extra plate. The apples need not be kept warm.
4. Serve celery hearts stuffed with cream cheese and chopped nuts or Roquefort

cheese; carrot sticks, pickles and olives in old fashioned glass containers made for that purpose. (Everybody has one or two such dishes stuck way back in the corner of the cupboard.)

5. Decorate ham platter with parsley.
6. Have shortcakes in individual bowls at end of sideboard.
7. Strong hot coffee, cream and sugar.

All the above should be placed on sideboard in an attractive manner. A bowl of beautiful fresh fruit will enhance the décor and appetite.

Will serve eight generously.

Roast Turkey, Oyster Dressing, and Brussels sprouts with water chestnuts, baked sweet potatoes, cranberry sauce, relishes, and persimmon pudding.

15-18 lb. turkey (a tom turkey, preferable fresh, has a very distinctive flavor, a hen tastes very much like chicken.)

Clean the turkey; take out the insides and cook the neck, all the giblets, except the liver, in 6 cups of water with one onion, large stalk of celery and salt.

1 – ½ loaves stale bread cubes.   ½ lb. sautéed mushroom
2 cups chopped celery   6 oysters (at least)
2 cups chopped onion
1 t salt and 1 t pepper, 1 T sage.

Soften celery and onion in a stick of butter before adding to the bread. Use meat from the neck and gizzard and combine this with the whole oysters which have been parboiled in their own juice until the edges curl. Add ½ lbs sautéed mushrooms. Add this to the bread mixture and additional seasoning if necessary. Now add the turkey stock to make a rather dry stuffing. It goes well with the oysters. Salt inside of bird. Stuff the turkey and sew it shut. Tie the feet. Rub bird with corn oil, salt and pepper it generously. Cover it with aluminum foil and bake at 375 for about 4 hours or longer if necessary. Baste the bird occasionally with the turkey stock. When the bird is done, remove the foil, baste it again and raise the temperature to 450 and brown the bird to a golden color.

Make gravy out of remaining stock and the brown stock in bottom of roaster. First skim off the grease. Then add 2 T flour, stirring constantly. Add another cup of stock and continue to stir and cook for another five minutes. Strain the gravy, add more stock or water if too thick and finally stir in ½ cup finely sliced cooked mushrooms.

Scrub yams and bake them the last two hours along with the turkey. Serve them sliced in half length wise, scored and buttered. (Be sure you buy yams.)

Cook frozen Brussels sprouts according to directions, adding butter and drained, sliced water chestnuts. Reheat.

Relishes: Stuffed celery hearts with Roquefort, carrot sticks, radishes, and ripe olives, sweet gherkins, all nicely chilled.

Persimmon Pudding: *(Here's where you get your money's worth. We've never tasted better!)*

Small Indiana Persimmons. One pint <u>frozen</u>, <u>thawed</u> persimmons. Put through a colander. Scrape bottom of colander with spatula so you get every bit of fruit. Add in given order:

½ t soda
2 eggs well beaten   Serve with
1 – ½ cups sugar   whipped cream or rum sauce, (although we prefer it plain.)
2 cups flour   Rum sauce: Cream in sauce-
1 t baking powder   pan ½ c butter, 2 c light brown sugar; add
3 cups milk   2 cups warm light cream.
3 t melted butter   Stir over low heat until it boils.
Butter Pyrex pan heavily.   Remove from heat add ½ cup rum. Beat with whisk.

Bake 1–½ hrs on top rack of oven at 275.

Serves 12.

Colleen's Sweat and Sour Pork
Rice
Tomatoes stuffed with cucumbers
Bread pudding

2-3 lbs. boned pork shoulder

Trim off fat, cut into small pieces and fry it slowly in skillet. Pour off fat and save for frying chicken, etc. The little brown cracklings are very tasty when salted and served with beer. If there are many pieces you may put them in the ricer to extract all fat, then break up the pieces and serve! *Give this to your hubby with his beer, as a snack* (Room temperature, don't refrigerate.)

Now for the meat; cut meat in medium size cubes, cook it in the greased skillet for 10 or 15 minutes until lightly browned. Cover with half sweet and sour sauce, as made by the Chinese, and half water. Cover and simmer for an hour. You can make your own sauce, but it involves quite a few ingredients and unnecessary work. I find the Chinese very satisfactory. Salt to taste. Serve over boiled rice. (*By now you should know that anything prepared under cover needs to be stirred every 15 or 20 minutes. And by all means, taste the fixings as you go along so you don't have any rude surprises.*)

Bread Pudding: 6 slices stale bread, butter, 3 eggs slightly beaten, ½ cup sugar, ¼ t salt, one quart milk.

Spread bread generously with butter, arrange in buttered pyrex dish, buttered side down. Add sugar, salt and milk to eggs, and pour over bread. Let stand 30 minutes. Bake one hour at 325. Cover the first half hour of baking. The top of pudding should be well browned. Serve with small scoop of vanilla ice cream on each helping.

Scoop out tomatoes and stuff with cubed cucumbers which have been salted and peppered.

Pork patties
Mashed potatoes
Green bean casserole
Bib lettuce/tomatoes and French dressing
Jello cheese cake with cherries

2 – 3 lbs. ground pork shoulder (this is the butt with the h-bone) ask the butcher to bone and grind it for you, (after you pick it out.) It might cost a little more per pound to have this done but it's worth it. 2 slices of excellent white bread per pound of ground pork.

1 egg per pound

1 t garlic powder per pound or mashed garlic salt and pepper

Soak bread in warm milk, add all ingredients except meat, and make it mushy. Now mix in the meat. Make half-inch thick generous patties, dip them in bread crumbs and fry them slowly in bacon drippings. Drain them on paper towels and keep warm.

Allow one medium potato per serving; peel potatoes, cook them until done. Drain them and shake the pan over heat so potatoes are dry. Add hot milk and mash them, adding salt and butter. Idaho's are the best for fluffy mashed potatoes.

Green Bean Casserole: 2 cans Del Monte green beans, not the French cut.
 2 cans cream of mushroom soup
 ½ can liquid off beans
 1 can French-friend onion rings

Mix beans, soup and liquid. Bake 30 minutes at 350. Top with onion rings and bake additional ten minutes.

Cheese cake made from scratch is a lot of work and quite costly. I find the packaged cake very satisfactory, easy to make and quite good. Before serving, spoon canned cherry pie filling or diluted blueberry jam over each serving.

Serves 8

Wiener Schnitzel
Gravy
Mashed potatoes
Honeyed carrots
3 bean salad apple fritter and syrup

8 slices boneless pork lion – about 2 lbs. salt, pepper, and flour

Place meat on board and flatten it with a mallet, easy, not paper thin. Salt and pepper on both sides. Then coat with flour. Pat the pieces so flour adheres. Heat 2-3 T butter in a skillet and cook over fairly high heat to brown lightly on one side, about 3-4 minutes. Turn and brown lightly on other side. Remove pieces to a dish and brown remaining schnitzels. Add more butter if necessary. Be careful to not allow butter to burn. When all the meat has been browned, put all in skillet and cover with cold water. Simmer this under cover for about an hour. Check to add more water if necessary, and/or loosen schnitzels from pan. Now add light cream with a tablespoon of flour mixed into it, to make gravy. Gravy will have bits of coating from the meat. Do not strain it. It's delicious. Add more flour with cream to have enough for the mashed potatoes. By all means taste the gravy. It should be peppery, and a tan color.

Mashed potatoes: One medium potato per serving, peeled and boiled until done. Rice the potatoes, add half a stick of butter, 1 tsp salt, and ½ c HOT milk. Add all ingredients to potatoes. Beat with fork until creamy, reheat and pile in hot dish.

Honeyed Carrots: Approximately one medium carrot per serving. Wash, peel and slice into pennies. Cover with water, add a tablespoon of butter, a teaspoon of honey and salt to taste. Cook quickly. Watch them carefully; add hot water if necessary. They will be done in 15-20 minutes. A small amount of liquid will be left in pan. Sprinkle with chopped parsley before serving.

3 bean salad: 1-16 oz can wax beans (drained)
1-16 oz can green beans (drained)
1-16 oz can kidney beans (drained)
½ cup thin rings sweet onion
½ green pepper, thin rings
½ cup salad oil
   ¾ cup sugar
½ cup vinegar   salt and pepper to taste
Make the day before: Place beans, onion and pepper rings in large bowl. Mix oil, sugar, vinegar, salt and pepper. Pour over beans and toss to coat. Cover and refrigerate for at

least 12 hours. Mix several times.

Apple Fritters: 1 cup flour, 1 ½ t baking powder, 3 T powdered sugar, ¼ t salt, 1/3 c milk, 1 egg, well beaten.

Mix and sift dry ingredients, add milk gradually and egg. 4 medium sour apples pared, cored, and cut in slices like doughnuts or cut in eighths. Stir into batter. Fry in hot corn oil 375-380 F, or until it is hot enough to brown an inch cube of bread in one minute. Dip a spoon into the fat, then take up a spoonful of the fritter mixture and carefully drop it into the fat. Fritters should be cooked through and delicately brown on the outside in three to five minutes. Remove with skimmer and drain on crumpled soft paper. *Apple fritters may be sprinkled with powdered sugar but we always liked them with maple syrup.*

Serves 4-6

Colleen's barbequed country ribs
Thick noodles
Green beans
Salad of water chestnuts
Apples celery coated sparingly with mild mayonnaise
Pineapple upside down cake

Buy two pieces of country ribs per adult serving. Wash and place them in 9 x 12 pan with ½ cup water, 1 t salt, in 350 oven for 30 minutes. Then pour off the liquid. Place onion rings over meat and homemade barbecue sauce over all. Cover with foil and bake for about an hour at 350.

Barbecue sauce:

1 t salt	¼ c brown sugar
1 c tomato ketchup	1 t chili powder
¼ c vinegar	2 c water
1 t celery seed	¼ c Worcestershire

Simmer half an hour.

Green beans: Follow directions on frozen pkg of beans, adding a lump of butter. If you are able to get tender, fresh green beans, cook them with two cut up, meaty slices of bacon or ham. Don't drown them. Just cover them with water and keep an eye on them. Shouldn't take more than 20 minutes.

Salad: Drain and rinse the water chestnuts. Slice them, add them to finely cut celery and apple. Serve in lettuce cups.

Pineapple upside down cake:

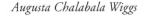
¼ cup butter	1 cup milk
½ cup sugar	2 ¼ cups flour
1 egg well beaten	4 t baking powder
½ t salt	

Cream butter, add sugar and egg; mix and sift flour with baking powder and salt. Add alternately with milk to first mixture. Turn into heavy frying pan which has been spread with 3 T butter, 3 T brown sugar and canned sliced pineapple. Bake in moderate oven 350 for about 35 minutes. Turn onto serving dish pineapple side up.

Chow mein
Noodles
Lime jello with cottage cheese
Stuffed olives
Almond cream

2 lbs. lean pork cut into ½" cubes	2 chicken bouillon cubes (or chicken broth)
2 t salt1 large green pepper	
4 T chopped onion	1 ½ c diced celery
2 large cloves garlic, crushed	2 T cornstarch
3 T oil	2 t soy sauce
¼ cup cold water	

Brown pork slowly in oil with onion, salt and garlic. Add two chicken bouillon cubes dissolved in one cup boiling water, cover and cook slowly for 20 minutes. Take a peak at it a couple of times to make sure everything is progressing nicely. Taste meat. Is it done? Now add the diced green pepper and celery. Cover and cook slowly five minutes. The pepper and celery will be crunchy and retain color. Blend the cornstarch, soy sauce, cold water and add to the meat. Cook until thick, stirring constantly. Pour over medium noodles (2 cups uncooked 8 oz) which have been cooked, drained, chilled, and then sautéed in 3 T oil. 4 generous servings.

Do this in the morning. Slice stuffed olives and lay in bottom of greased pyrex bread pan. Over this, spoon cottage cheese. Dissolve lime jello (3 oz.) When jello is mushy, spoon/pour over the cottage cheese and allow to jell completely. When ready to serve, invert on small platter, cut into serving pieces and serve on lettuce leaf with dab of mayonnaise. Make in cake mold for buffet. (Double entire menu for buffet)

Almond Cream: Serve in stemmed glasses or clear sherbets

2 cups half and half	One envelope unflavored gelatin
2 tsp almond extract	One cup cold water
1 can 11 oz mandarin oranges	

Sprinkle gelatin over water in a pan; let stand five minutes to soften. Place over medium heat and stir until dissolved. Add sugar and stir until dissolved. Remove from heat and stir in half and half and almond extract. Pour into serving dishes and chill until firm – at least 4 hours. To serve, drain chilled oranges and decorate the cream. *This is a very elegant and exotic dessert. Don't waste it on a heavy smoker or drinker.*

Hungarian Goulash
Dumplings
Brussels sprouts
Sauerkraut
Onions and cukes in sour cream

2-3 lbs. pork, large onion, ½ small can tomato sauce (or tomato juice), medium can sauerkraut.

Paprika and salt

Cut up pork into one inch chunks and wash meat. (If you have plants, wash meat in dish pan and our the water on plants.) Fry sliced onion in couple T of bacon drippings until limp. Add pork, sprinkle 1 T paprika over it, and cover. Allow to simmer for 15 minutes. Then add 1 t salt, the tomato sauce and water, mix thoroughly, cover and let stew for 2 hours, stirring every thirty minutes or so. If stew gets dry, add HOT water. The last half hour, add drained and rinsed sauerkraut. The stew should not be runny but have a nice thick sauce. If necessary, sprinkle 1 T of flour into it or couple T's of corn starch.

Serve with dumplings and Brussels sprouts. If it's a meal for men, make cucumbers with sour cream, and serve beer with meal.

Dumplings: Home made is best, but if you're tired, use refrigerator biscuits place on top of stew, covered and steam for 12 minutes. Tear biscuits in half with forks to allow steam to escape before serving.

Dumplings from Scratch:

Beat 2 eggs in a bowl, add 1 c milk, 1 t butter, salt and enough flour to make a thick dough which can be beaten thoroughly with a wooden spoon. Beat five or more minutes until the dough is satiny, then let it rest half an hour. In the meantime fry two slices of bread in butter cook and cut into cubes add to dough. Make dumplings the size of a small apple, dust your hands with flour and roll each into a round ball. Place in boiling salted water and boil ten minutes. They may stick when dumplings are placed in water, so pry them loose with a wooden spoon. Cover tightly and boil for five minutes. They must boil constantly but not rapidly. After five or six minutes, raise lid and with couple of spoons turn dumplings over, cover again and continue to cook for another 5-6 minutes. When done, tear each dumpling apart with two forks to make them light and airy.

Ham Loaf
Scalloped potatoes
Frozen Squash
Green beans
Monkey bread
Fresh fruit compote.

1 lb. ground ham*
1 lb. fresh pork*
1 c dry bread crumbs (not cracker crumbs)
2 eggs
1 c milk

Combine all ingredients thoroughly. Pack lightly into a 9 x 5 x 3 inch loaf pan.

Bake at 350 for one hour.

*Pick out the cuts of meat to grind. If the butcher is reluctant to do this, speak to the manager. As an alternative, triple the amount and freeze two loaves.

Allow frozen squash to defrost. Add a generous tablespoon of butter and one teaspoon of brown sugar, salt & pepper and heat. Serve on same plate with ham loaf.

Cook frozen green beans as per directions, adding lump of butter and salt.

Monkey Bread: Refrigerated crescent rolls; cut triangles into two triangles. Dip in melted butter and lay around ring mold. Bake at 350 until brown. Serve on platter and let people tear off pieces. Very Yummy.

Fresh Fruit Compote: Watermelon balls, cantaloupes balls, honeydew balls, sliced strawberries and fresh blueberries or pitted Bing cherries. Do not add blueberries or cherries until just before serving because they'll darken the syrup and other fruits. Pour simple syrup over these.

Simple Syrup: 1c sugar, 2 c water boiled for two or three minutes. You may add a few mint leaves to compote for flavor, or simply add one-two leaves of mint for decoration. Serve in fruit dishes and a spoon.

The fruit compote can be made in the morning and refrigerated.

Scalloped Potatoes: 4 potatoes, pared & cut in ¼" slices.

Salt & pepper

Flour for dredging

2 T butter, milk

Put layer of potatoes in buttered baking dish, sprinkle with s & p and dredge with flour; dot\ over with half the butter; repeat. Add milk until it may be seen though top layer. Bake 1-1/4 hrs in mod over 350 or until potatoes are soft. (at the same time as ham loaf.)

Serves 6.

Note: baked squash, no potatoes necessary, the starch is in the monkey bread, ok?

Pork Goulash with boiled potatoes
Wilted Lettuce Salad
Coffee
Little Drunkards - Cookies

Goulash:

2-1/2 lbs. pork shoulder	½ c water
3 T butter	1 T paprika
2 onions	1 lb sauerkraut
1 t caraway	½ c sour cream
1 clove crushed garlic	
1 T dill salt & pepper	

Fry onions in butter until limp. Add the crushed garlic and the cut up meat. Swizzle this until all coated, then add caraway, dill, salt & pepper, and paprika. Cover and allow to simmer for about 15-20 minutes. Now add the water. Cover and let stew for about two hours, stirring every half hour or so. Add hot water or broth as needed.

When meat is almost done, add one large can of DelMonte sauerkraut. We find it the best. Drain and rinse the kraut before adding it to the meat. When all is done, mix in the sour cream. Remember this is a stew – there must be broth. If it's too runny, add a couple of spoons of instant potatoes. Add broth if too thick. Rye bread & butter with this.

Boil white potatoes, one for each serving, and serve with the stew.

Wilted Lettuce Salad:

Wash and dry a head of lettuce and tear into shreds. Arrange the lettuce in salad bowl. Dice 4 slices bacon and sauté them until crisp. Drain them on paper. To the fat remaining in pan, add 3 T vinegar, 2 T sugar, a bit of salt and dry mustard. Pour the dressing over the lettuce, toss it well and sprinkle it with the diced bacon. Serve immediately.

Little Drunkards:

1 c butter	2/3 c sugar
½ t salt	2 egg yolks
3 c sifted flour	¼ c claret or other wine
cinnamon-sugar	

Cream butter and sugar. Add salt and egg yolks; mix well. Add flour alternately with wine. Shape into small balls between the palms. Flatten each cookie with the bottom of a glass dipped in sugar and cinnamon. Bake at 375 deg for about 10 mins, and sprinkle while hot with more cinnamon and sugar.

BUFFET DINNER
(Time – approximately three (3) hrs.)

Baked Ham (precooked)
Baked Yams (one for each serving)
Green Beans (1 – ½ lbs. or 2 pkgs frozen)
Fried Apples (3 to 4 apples cored and sliced)
Rolls & Biscuits (in half inch slices)
Blueberry or Strawberry Shortcake
Salad – celery hearts, carrot sticks, olives
Coffee

Skin ham (save skin), cut off most of fat (save this for making ham drippings and cracklings*.) Score the ham, and rub with 1 c brown sugar, 2 T vinegar, and 1 T mustard mixed; insert one clove in each diamond. Place fat side up in uncovered pan at 325 deg for two hrs. This is enough time for about half a ham. An entire precooked ham should be baked longer.

Scrub yams and bake at same time as ham – allowing 1 ½ to 2 hrs at 325 deg.

Bake biscuits in the morning and keep them covered so they won't dry out.

Cook beans according to directions and add 2 T butter.

Core apples and slice them. Omit ends. Sprinkle with sugar and fry them in butter, turning once until soft; add drop of lemon juice if apples are not tart.

For dessert, use two biscuits for each serving of shortcake.

Add about half c water to jar of blueberry or strawberry preserves and heat. If you're lucky enough to have fresh fruit, mash half with sugar and add whole berries to remainder. Spoon berries over biscuits and top with whipped cream.

1.Slice ham in kitchen and place on sideboard.

2.Cut yams in half & score them, adding salt and butter to each.

3.Warm rolls in oven after removing ham and yams. Put rolls into serving dish on white napkin and cover to keep warm.

4.Put beans into hot covered vegetable dish and apples on extra plate. The apples need not be kept warm.

5.Serve celery hearts stuffed with cream cheese and chopped nuts, carrot sticks, pickles and olives in old fashioned glass containers made for that purpose.

6.Decorate ham platter with parsley.

7.Strong hot coffee, cream & sugar.

8.Have shortcakes in individual bowls at end of sideboard.

All the above should be place on sideboard in an attractive manner. A bowl of beautiful fresh fruit will enhance the décor and appetite.

Will serve eight generously.

About the ham skin and ham fat -
Our kids used to like the skins boiled with potatoes; chewy and tasty.
The ham fat rendered is very good mixed with bacon drippings or lard for frying meats.
Cut the ham fat into small pieces, place them into a small pot and put on back of range
on low heat until all fat has been rendered. The ham fat will be pure white. Now put the
remnants of the fat into a ricer and squeeze the remainder of the fat. Yummy! Now you have
cracklings.

Lentils with boiled beef
Rye bread & butter
Egg dumplings
Lemon Jello
Apple pie

Ingredients:
2 cups lentils
2 lbs. beep rump
1 med. Onion
S& P
Thyme, vinegar and water

Dumplings
½ cup butter
2 eggs
2 cups flour
½ t salt
2/3 cup milk

Lemon Jello
1 cup grated carrot
1 cup sliced celery
3 oz. pkg. lemon jello

Pie crust

Wash lentils in cold water and soak a couple of hrs. Lentils swell to twice their size while boiling, so if you put two cups of lentils to boil, you will need a quart pan. Drain off the water in which the lentils have soaked and cover with fresh water and boil gently for 45 mins. Brown the onion lightly in lard or bacon drippings and add it to the lentils. Also a bit of powdered thyme. Thicken with flour and butter browned together. Add vinegar and water to taste.

Boiled beef: Rump is best used for boiled beef but it must not be too fat. Place beef n salted boiling water, cover well, and simmer gently. The meat must be simmered until it is easily pierced with a fork. If boiled too long it crumbles and loses flavor. If boiled rapidly, it will be tough. Boiled beef is cut into medium slices.

Egg dumplings: ½ cup softened butter and 2 eggs beaten until creamy. Stir in 2 cups flour and ½ t salt. Add to this gradually about 2/3 cups milk until a firm batter is formed. Cut out the batter with a soup spoon which has been dipped in cold water each time, and drop the batter into boiling water. Reduce the liquid to a simmer, cover and cook for about 12 mins. After the first 6 min. uncover and turn dumplings with two spoons and continue cooking covered for an additional 6-8 minutes. Drain. Add additional dumplings one at a time so they don't stick. Stir with a wooden spoon. If dumplings stick to bottom of pan, pry them loose with a wooden spoon. Serve with lentils and boiled beef. In the morning make apple pie. Bake pie late in the day so it will be warm for dinner.

Pie crust: 1 cup lard, ½ cup boiling water, 1 t salt, 3 cups flour. Place lard in a warm bowl and break it up into small pieces. Add salt and hot water and stir with a fork until creamy. Add flour and stir only to blend. Chill one hour before using. (This will keep in the refrigerator for a week). Will make enough dough for 1 double crust pie & 1 shell depending on size. Line pie plate with paste. Pare, core & cut 6-8 sour apples in eights; put row around plate ½ inch from edge, and work towards the center until plate is covered; then pile on remainder. Mix ½ to ¾ cup sugar, ¼ t nutmeg or cinnamon, ¼ t salt, ½ T butter and 2 t lemon juice if apples aren't tart enough. Wet edges of under crust, cover with upper crust, and press edges together. Set pie in bottom of hot oven 450 for 10 minutes, then move to middle shelf, reduce heat to 350 and bake 40- 45 min.

Peas, barley and Ham
Sliced tomatoes
Fruit cup
Rye bread and butter

Ingredients:
2 cups dried yellow peas (in shells) 1 cup pearl barley, large Spanish onion
3 lbs. smoked butt, boneless (daisy brand type is very nice)

Cook smoked meat until tender. This usually takes about 1- ½ hrs. Pick over peas and wash in cold water. Soak in cold water overnight or for 4-6 hrs. Drain off water and cover with fresh water, and cook until soft. Two cups will make at least four cups of peas. Add hot water as needed. Salt after cooking.

Meanwhile rinse barley, add 3 cups cold water and 1 t salt, cover and cook slowly until tender, about 50 minutes. More hot water may have to be added during cooking, depending on the size of grain. Peas will take about the same amount of time. Slice and fry onion in bacon drippings combined with equal amt of butter.

Combine peas and barley and pour fried onion with drippings over all. Slice smoked meat, place around mound of peas and barley and serve. Delicious! A real cold weather dish. Very substantial. Pass rye bread and butter.

Peel tomatoes and slice. Sprinkle with salt and pepper.

Canned sliced raggedy Anne peaches(chilled)

Red beans and rice
Broiled tomatoes parmesan
Apple sauce
Beer
Chocolate ice cream sundae
Compliments of Camille Osborn!

Ingredients:
One lb. red beans
1-2 med onions
3-6 cloves minced garlic
2-3 cut up stalks celery
½ lb. lean salt pork cut into small slices
1 T chili powder or 2 t cumin (season to taste really) black rough ground pepper
2 lbs. smoked sausage (Ekrich if you can get it) one cup raw rice
6-8 med. Firm tomatoes
½ c miracle whip
½ c minced onion
½ c parmesan cheese
Soak red beans overnight, then drain.

Fry sliced salt pork in one spoon of butter, then add all the other ingredients and frizzle together. Add the drained soaked beans, cover with HOT water. Bring to a boil; lower to simmer for 2-1/2 hrs. STIR every 30 minutes.

After two hours take fork and mashed the cooked beans against the side of the pot so it becomes quite thick.

Add sliced smoked sausage at the last (or cook two meaty hams hocks in it.)

DO NOT SALT. The salt pork and/or ham are enough.

Serve over cooked rice. *Unbelievable flavor!*
Serve broiled tomatoes parmesan:
Peel tomatoes, cut in half and salt lightly.
Place on foil-lined broiler pan.
Add dollops of miracle, minced onion, and parmesan cheese all mixed together.
Put under broiler 3-5 minutes until puffy. Serve immediately
A hearty meal like this calls for a cold bottle of beer. So serve it.
Chocolate ice cream sundae for dessert.
Four to six generous servings.

Menus Featuring Chicken

Ladies Luncheon Bridge Party
Macaroni-chicken casserole
Stuffed tomato, salad, sauterne jelly
iced tea
a glass of sherry for the ladies before lunch. We like Taylor's.

Fry one small onion. Leave skin chicken thighs, drum sticks and/or breasts on and do not bone the pieces. They add great flavor to the cream sauce. Salt and pepper all sides. Put pieces into frying pan, cover and simmer (medium heat) for half hour. After half hour, turn pieces and sauté other side for 30 minutes. There will about a quarter cup (or more) chicken fat with lovely juices. Remove the chicken. Add two to three tablespoon of flour, stirring constantly for 2-3 minutes. Gradually add water, or chicken soup, to roux. Continue stirring and adding stock until you have at least a cup or more sauce. *Do not add milk; it looks too anemic when you add the precooked seashells.*

Precook seashells (the small ones) for five minutes. In the meantime skin and debone chicken. The meat will almost fall off the bones. Now cut meat into good size pieces, mix into sauce, then add drained precooked sea shells and half a cup of slivered almonds. Pour mixture into greased Pyrex dish. Bake in hot oven for 20 minutes under cover. Remove cover and continue to bake for another 15-20 minutes. Sprinkle chopped parsley over all. Serve hot.

Stuffed tomato salad: peel medium sized tomatoes, one per person. Remove thin slice from top of each and take out seeds and some of pulp. Sprinkle inside with salt; invert and let stand one half hour. Fill tomatoes with equal parts of apple and celery, finely cut, mixed with mayonnaise. Serve on shredded lettuce.

Sauterne - orange jello: Add 1 cup of boiling water to dissolve orange gelatin. Then add ½ cup sauterne and ½ cup cold water. Fill sherbet glasses with cooled gelatin with ¾ of the mixture. The remainder, after cooling, is to be beaten until frothy and piled on top.

Coconut cookies:
1c butter
1c sugar
1 egg
½ t vanilla
½ t baking soda
2c flour
¼ cup water or rum

Cream coconut butter and sugar. Add beaten egg and vanilla. Sift flour and soda and add to creamed mixture with water or rum. Roll in wax paper in 4, eight inch rolls & rerig for half hr. or longer (next day). Cut into ¼" chunks and bake on greased cookie sheet for 10 mins at 350. Makes a lot.

Serves 4 gererously. Double if you have two tables of bridege.

BRIDGE LUNCHEON
Chicken salad
Apple
Celery
Few Thompson grapes
Mayonnaise
Biscuits with homemade jam
White wine

Cook chicken in boiling water with cut up celery, onion, and salt in only enough water to cover. If it's a 3 lb chicken, it will be done in one hr. simmer only long enough to cook chicken so chicken retains its' flavor- you are not making chicken soup. Allow to cool in broth. Skin, bone and cut all parts of chicken. Add one cup celery cut in small pieces, one small apple cut in small pieces (golden grimes is nice or bosc pear). If you can find them in the market, a half cup of Thompson grapes is very good. *Don't use those big green ones.* Add one T of finely cut onion to salad. Mix all ingredients with mayonnaise which has been thinned with cream or ½ & ½, about one cup of dressing with 2 T cream. Serve in lettuce cups. Pass tiny biscuits, either home baked or refrigerator type which have been cut in half, brushed with butter and a light sprinkling of sugar and homemade strawberry jam.

Biscuits: 2 cups flour	3 T lard
4 t baking powder	about I c milk
½ t salt	

Mix dry ingredients and sift. Work in shortening with pastry mixer. Add liquid gradually, mixing with fork or wooden spoon to soften dough. Toss on floured board, pat, and roll lightly ½ inch thick. Shape with small biscuit cutter. Place on greased cookie sheet, brush with melted butter and sprinkle lightly with sugar. Bake 12- 15 min in hot oven 450. The amt of liquid may vary slightly due to differences in flour.

Strawberry jam:
Two quarts berries
3 lbs. sugar or 7 cups sur –jell yield about 8 ½ cups

Wash glasses and lids and drain.

Crush fully ripe berries, one layer at a tme, so that each berry is reduced to a pulp. A potato masher is good for this. Mix in sugar.

Mix sure-jell with fruit in saucepan (use aluminum or porcelain pan so berries don't lose tartness). Place over high heat and stir until mixture comes to a FULL boil. Boil hard one minute, stirring constantly. Remove from heat; skim off foam with metal spoon. Stir and skim five minutes to cool slightly.

Ladle into glasses, leaving ½ inch space at top. Cover jam immediately with 1/8 inch ht paraffin. Cool and cover with loose fitting lids.

(complete instructions come in Sure-Jell box. You will need two large kettles; one for crushing and one for preparing fruit, a metal spoon, a large mouth funnel and tongs. Always sterilize jars).

More about strawberry jam: it can be used on strawberry sundaes or shortcake. Empty jam into pan, add ¼ cup water, heat and stir. Do not boil. In a pretty jar, jam makes a proper and unique "bread and butter" gift.

Creamed Chicken with Mushrooms
Little dumplings
Shredded carrot with raisins, mayonnaise
Peas with pearl onions
Chocolate mousse

Cut up one 3 ½ # chicken. Save neck, back and gizzard for stock pot. Place chicken into pan with butter and cover with ½ # sliced mushrooms. Cook under cover for a few minutes and then add about two cups hot water or soup (soup is better), salt, cover and stew until done about an hour, not uncovering pan too much. Then take meat out and thicken gravy with flour, add two or three sprigs of chopped parsley. Let this simmer for awhile. Add half and half, enough to make gravy of nice consistency. Place meat in center of platter and surround with little dumplings and decorate with parsley.

Dumplings:

¼ lb. butter, 4 eggs, 1- ¾ c sifted flour, ½ t salt. Cream the butter until light and fluffy. Add the eggs one at a time, beating well after each. Sift the flour and salt together and add to previous mixture. Mix well and shape into a long thin roll. Set aside for 15 min. break off very small pieces and drop into either salted water or boiling soup. Remove the dumplings as they come to the top, which should be in about 3 min. Place in colander to drain. Serve hot. Pore some of the gravy over dumplings. Pass extra gravy at table.

Chocolate mousse: jello chocolate fudge pudding. Prepare as directed. Fold in 1/3 cup pecans cut in good sized pieces. Do this while the pudding is hot. When pudding has cooled completely, fold in one pint of whipped cream. Ladle into sherbet glasses and refrigerate until ready to serve. (Just for looks; it adds nothing to the flavor, believe me, which is heavenly).

Pkg. of frozen peas cooked with 2 T butter. Buy the canned pearl onions, or the frozen peas and onions. Cook as directed on package. If you use the canned onions, drain them and add them to the hot peas. Do not cook but bring up to heat.

Serves 4-6

Spring menu
CHICKEN PILAF
Chicken pilaf with mushrooms and rice
Peas and carrots
Wedge of lettuce with 1,000 island dressing
Apricot mousse

Ingredients:
Two whole chicken breasts and four thighs (or 2 # chicken parts)
½ # fresh mushrooms
1 ½ cups rice
one pkg. frozen peas
½ # carrots
head of lettuce
6 oz. pkg. apricot jello
1 med. can Del Monte apricots

1 plump young chicken cut up for frying (or divided chicken breasts and thighs). Season with s&p and brown lightly in butter or chicken fat. Now pour2 cups of chicken bouillon over it, add a pinch of saffron, 1T parsley, ½ t sage & thyme, cover pot and let simmer(the saffron can be omitted). Wash and cook rice in boiling well-salted water for five minutes; drain and then add to the chicken along with washed, sliced mushrooms. Cover and cook over slow fire until rice is done, about 15 minutes. Add the rice after chicken has been simmering for 40-45 minutes. *Delicious.*

Peel and slice carrots; cover with water which has a little salt and ½ t honey. Cook until fork tender. Add 2 T butter and uncooked peas. Cook only long enough to heat the peas. *They are delicious and taste fresh out of the garden.(keep an eye on the carrots so they don't burn. Stir them frequently and add hot water if needed, but don't drown them).*

Dissolve jello and allow to jell. If you re using canned apricots which have been strained or put in blender, substitute the syrup for an equal amt. of water in the jello. When jello has jelled, add strained apricots and allow to jell further. Before it reaches a firm jell, fold in whipped cream. Spoon this into sherbet glasses, allowing it to set completely. *Lovely in the spring.*

This will serve four to six people.

Chicken paprika
Rice
Asparagus
Grapefruit salad
Tapioca pudding

Ingredients:

Chicken parts without backs or necks equivalent to 2-3 # chicken

Medium onion

1 cup Sour cream, 3 cups cooked rice, one cup chicken stock (made from skin, backs and necks)

1 ½ T sweet paprika

Draw out fat from chicken carcass and render it so you have two T of fat. Skin the chicken; salt all the pieces, brown them lightly in the fat remove pieces as they brown and add sliced onion. Cook onion until lightly colored. Off the heat stir in the paprika, stirring until the onion is well coated. Return the skillet to the heat and add the chicken stock. Bring to a boil, and return chicken to the skillet. Cover pan and simmer the chicken for approximately 30 min, stirring once or twice. When the chicken is done, remove it to a platter. Skim the surface fat from the skillet. In a mixing bowl, stir the flour into the sour cream with a fork or wire whisk, then add the mixture to the simmering juices. Simmer six- eight minutes longer until sauce is thick and smooth, then return chicken to pan. Baste with the sauce and simmer a couple of minutes to heat the pieces through, and serve.

Rice: bring 3 cups of water to boil. add 1 ½ cups rice and 1 t salt, plus 1 T butter. Mix with fork. Cover closely and simmer 20-25 min. until rice is cooked and has absorbed all the liquid.

Cook the asparagus according to directions on pkg. and add 2 T butter, nothing else.

Peel oranges, removing as much of the white membrane as possible and slice. Peel grapefruit, segment it, and remove tough fiber from sections. Arrange orange slices and grapefruit sections and thinly sliced sweet purple onions on lettuce and dribble mayonnaise thinned with grapefruit juice over fruit.

Make tapioca according to directions on box. *Do this in the morning. A dollop of whipped cream on each serving sprinkled with a bit of nutmeg is very nice.*

Chicken and pork rice
Italian green beans
Romaine lettuce and radish salad with Italian dressing
Pecan pie

Ingredients
Half pound pork sausage links, cut in chunks
One three pound frying chicken, cut up
One 15 oz can Hunt's special tomato sauce
One cup water
¾ cups raw regular rice
1t salt
1 clove garlic minced
Two T grated parmesan cheese

Brown sausage, and remove. In the same skillet brown chicken; remove and drain fat, add remaining ingredients (except the cheese) to skillet, and stir. Return sausage and chicken. Cover and simmer 35-40 minutes.

Sprinkle with cheese. Serves 4-6

Pecan pie:

½ c up granulated sugar
One cup dark corn syrup
Three eggs
4 T butter
1 cup whole pecan halves
1 T vanilla
1 9- inch unbaked pastry shell

Cook syrup and sugar until mixture thickens. Beat eggs without separating. Add hot syrup to the eggs slowly, continuing to beat, and then add butter, vanilla and nuts. Pour into the unbaked pie shell and bake in hot oven for 10 min. at 450, then at 300 for 30 minutes longer. Cool and serve with or without whipped cream.

Fried chicken
Cauliflower with peas
Scraped new red potatoes
Lemon jello with carrots and celery
Pineapple Rice Bavarian

Ingredients:
Two frying chickens, approx. 3 lbs. each
Bread crumbs- two eggs
Large head cauliflower
One box frozen peas
Small new red potatoes- about two per person
One small can pineapple, crushed
One large can pineapple slices
Two cups cooked rice
Juice of one lemons
Two cups sugar syrup (1 c sugar boiled with 1 cup water)
One ½ oz gelatin pkg.
Two cups whipped cream

Method of preparation:

Buy chickens on Thursday or Friday when newly delivered at market, and cut up. Allow at least two pieces per person. Use entire chicken or just breast, thigh and drumsticks.

Rinse, dry with paper towels only moderately so salt & pepper will stick. Have four utensils ready: 1. cookie sheet 2. large mixing bowl for bread crumbs and cracker meal 3. flat soup bowl for flour, and 4. another bowl for beaten eggs.

Home made bread crumbs are best. However commercial crumbs mixed with equal parts of cracker meal and graham crackers are the best.

Lay chicken pieces on cookie sheet, s&p meat on both sides. Put about one cup of four in one bowl beat two eggs with equal amounts of water in other bowl.

Pour mix of bread crumbs and cracker meal into mixing bowl.

Now coat each piece of chicken with flour, patting each piece to make flour adhere to meat. Shake off excess flour. Do this with all pieces. Dip each piece into beaten egg, then into bowl with crumbs. Again make sure each piece is completely covered with bread mixture, putting it between palms of you hands for firm coating and shaking off any excess.

Melt one pound of lard or half lard and half bacon drippings (this is better) in large aluminum frying pan or an electric pan. To test for proper heat, drop few crumbs into pan. When they sizzle, the temperature is right for frying. Place breaded chicken pieces into hot fat (med. or 340 in electric pan). Chicken pieces should be half deep in fat. Don't crowd them. Cover and cook for 12- 15 min. depending on size of pieces. Remove lid QUICKLY and try not to let moisture from lid drip into fat because it will spit. Turn pieces with tongs or a pancake turner and fork(which I prefer) without piercing meat. If the pieces stick to bottom of pan, use your spatula or pancake turner for loosening. Cover again and continue cooking for another 12-15 minutes. Each time watch that dripping lid! Drain on double thickness of paper towels and keep warm in oven on VERY LOW temp.

Add more paper towels as additional layers of chicken are added to dish. If towels become saturated with the fat, replace them with fresh ones.

For homemade bread crumbs, buy day old Fr.. Bread, cut into slices, place on cookie sheet in slow oven. When dried out, mash in blender two slices at a time.

Trim cauliflower, leaving it in a nest of delicate green leaves. Place in a kettle of boiling chicken broth, well seasoned. If you have one of those old strainers which used to be used for frying potatoes, set the cauliflower in this. Cover the kettle and cook until cauliflower is done, firm and not mushy (25 mins) test by inserting knife into top of head. It should go in with ease. Raise strainer,, allowing cauliflower to drip, or remove to a bwl with two slotted spoons; don't break the head. Pour box of frozen (or fresh) peas barely cooked, over cauliflower and pour melted butter over all. When serving, cut head into eight sections(like a pie), serving individual pieces with a spoonful of peas and butter. *Delicious and very attractive. (discard soup or pour some on the dog's food. It's very attractive but smells funny.)* Or you can make a cream of cauliflower soup by merely thickening it with flour and milk.

Salad; grate carrots and finely sliced celery into mushy lemon jello and allow to set. Serve with mayonnaise thinned with milk or ½ and ½ .

Potatoes: new red potatoes are best in spring and early summer. Allow two for each serving. Wash and put them in a bowl of cold water. With a knife, scrape off skin. This may take about 20 minutes. Drain potatoes under running water. Add salt and a teaspoon of caraway seeds. Cover and cook over moderate heat for about 20 mins. Don't overcook. When done, drain and pour melted butter and chopped parsley and serve.

Scrape potatoes while chicken is frying. It will not hurt flavor of potatoes if they rest in cold water for half an hour or so.

In the morning: prepare the salad and the dessert.

Pineapple Rice Bavarian

1 cup canned crushed pineapple

2 cups sugar syrup (1 c water + 1 c sugar)

2 cups cooked rice

one ½ oz pkg gelatin (knox)

2 cups whipped cream

8 pineapples slices, fresh if possible

juice of one lemon

Mix crushed fruit with sugar syrup and cooked rice. Add lemon juice, and dissolved gelatin. When almost gelled, fold in whipped cream. Pour in mold well oiled with sweet almond oil (if possible). Chill till set. Turn out and arrange pineapple around rice. Serves 4-6

This is an exceptionally tasty and attractive meal. The oftener you do it, the easier and tastier it becomes. Don't be discouraged if the chicken is not perfect. If you are not certain whether or not to turn the chicken pieces in the pan, the uncooked part of the chicken should show juices and even to a small degree, spots of blood. This indicates that the bottom half is done and meat should be turned. The done side also becomes moist to indicate doneness.

You may have flour and egg left over from breading. Mix these together, adding more flour or water to make consistency of batter. Fry cakes of this in the drippings from the chicken. The drippings have been flavored by the chicken. You may get 3 or 4 small pancakes. Delicious sliced into shoestrings and added to soup.

Individual Recipes
for Odds and Ends

Chicken cacciatore
Dilled peas and cucumber
Crab newsburg
No more green yolks
Baked lima beans in tomato sauce

1 large chicken or 4-6 chicken breasts	1 can stewed tomatoes
2 T olive oil	1- 1 ½ cups sliced mushrooms
1 med. garlic clove	velveeta cheese
1 t oregano	ripe & stuffed green olives

Pan brown chicken in oil with garlic. Before turning chicken, sprinkle with oregano, s&p. Remove garlic. Add mushrooms, cook slightly. Add stewed tomatoes; cover, simmer 30-45 min. uncover and continue cooking till sauce is reduced to consistency desired and chicken is tender. Add Velveeta and 8-10 sliced ripe olives and some stuffed green olives before serving. Garnish with parsley. Serve over green noodles. Serves 4.

Dilled peas and cucumber

In a small saucepan cook a 10 oz. pkg frozen peas just until done. Drain. Meanwhile, peel a small cucumber, then quarter lengthwise. With a spoon scoop out seeds from each quarter; cut into ½ inch slices. In medium skillet melt one T butter. Add cucumbers and ¼ t dillweed; sauté 1 min. Add peas to cucumbers and toss until mixed. Heat and serve.

Crab newburg

In large skillet melt 4 t butter. Add a green or red pepper, seeded and coarsely chooped, and ¼ lb slice mushrooms; sauté about 5 mins. Stir in 2 T flour and cook 1 min. stirring constantly. Add 1- ½ cups milk (cold) a little at a time and continue stirring until sauce is smooth and thickened. Add 3 T dry sherry and ¼ t salt. Add one lb. frozen "sea legs" (imitation crab legs) cut diagonally into one inch slices. Simmer just until crab is heated through, about 2-3 min. serve over hot cooked rice.

No more green yolks- for perfect hardcooked eggs; place in saucepan in single layer; cover with cold water. Bring to just boil. turn off heat; cover and let stand 15 mins. Drain and immerse in cold water to stop cooking. Refrigerate.

Baked lima beans in tomato sauce

1 pk (1 lb) large dried limas	2 t dry mustard
9 slices bacon	2 t Worchester sauce
1 cup chopped onion	½ t oregano
1 can (8 oz) tomato sauce	¼ cup light brown sugar firmly packed

Soak beans overnight. Preheat oven to 350. In large bowl, combine beans, sautéed onion and 5 slices bacon, tomato sauce, reserved bean liquid, brown sugar, dry mustard, Worchester sauce and oregano. Mix until ingredients are well blended. Turn into 2 ½ quart shallow baking dish. Bake covered 30 mins. Remove cover and bake 15 min. longer. Meanwhile sauté remaining four slices bacon until crisp. Drain on paper towel. Arrange bacon slices over beans before serving. Makes 8 servings.

Ham and Corn Fritters

1 cup minced cooked ham	¼ t paprika
1 can corn	2 eggs
1 cup flour	1 t baking powder
1 t salt	

Drain corn and add dry ingredients, mixed and sifted, then add ham and yolks of eggs beaten until thick. Fold in stiffly beaten egg whites. Cook in frying pan in hot fat, drain on paper. Serve with maple syrup. Serves 6

Stuffed Pork chops and dressing

8 lean pork chops	¼ cup chopped celery
8 slices toasted bread	1 egg
1 small chopped onion	salt and pepper

Use stale toasted bread; moisten with water until bread holds together. Add onion, egg, chopped celery, salt and pepper. Spread dressing on 4 pork chops, top with another chop, sandwiching the dressing in between. Bake until pork chops are tender in moderate oven, about one hour. Serves 4.

Steak and Kidney Pie

2 lbs. top round steak	1 t salt
3 veal kidneys	1 t freshly ground pepper
1 t crushed rosemary leaves	flour
6 t butter	1 t tomato paste
2 med onions sliced very thin	1 cup red wine
½ lb. sliced mushrooms	puff paste

Cut round steak into 2" cubes. Trim the fat from the kidneys and cut them into small cubes. Dredge the steak and kidneys in the flour and sear them quickly in the hot butter. Add onions to the hot fat and let them cook until just soft. In a deep baking dish arrange the meat, onions and sliced mushrooms. Mix pepper, rosemary, tomato past, cognac or wine together and pour over the meat. Cover the dish and bake in 350 oven for approximately 2 hours, adding more wine if the liquid gets too low (or beef broth). While meat is cooking, prepare puff paste or biscuit dough. Roll the dough out into a rectangle ½" thick. Chill for 20 mins. Then roll the dough into a circle 2" larger than the top of the baking dish containing the meat. Place the dough on top of meat stew; make several slits for steam to escape and bake at 450 for ten mins. Serves 6.

German potato salad

8 slices bacon	4 t salt
3 T flour	½ t pepper
4 t chopped onion	1 t dry mustard
2/3 cup vinegar	½ t crumbled rosemary leaves
½ cup sugar	2 qts. Cooked diced potatoes
2/3 cup water	½ cup chopped fresh parsley.

Fry bacon until crisp. Remove from pan, drain and crumble. Add flour and onion to the bacon fat. Stir in vinegar, water, sugar, salt and spices. Cook until mixture is of medium thickness. Add to potatoes, parsley and crumbled bacon. Mix carefully to prevent mashing the potatoes. Serves 8-10

WARM THE PLATES

Coconut Cream Pie (Ann's)

Mix 2 c milk and one cup sugar in double boiler. Bring water to a boil. Blend 3 beaten egg yolks and two heaping T cornstarch and add to the mixture in the boiler. Boil until thick, about 3-4 minutes stirring all the time to prevent lumping. Then remove from the heat, add 4 T butter, ¼ t salt, 1 t vanilla and one cup coconut. Cool. Pour it into a 9" baked pie shell. Top with one cup whipped cream and decorate with coconut.

Borrachitos (Little Drunkards) (Bert's)

1 c butter or shortening	2/3 c sugar
½ t salt	2 egg yolks
3 cups sifted flour	¼ c claret or other wine
cinnamon-sugar	

Cream butter and sugar. Add salt and egg yolks; mix well. Add flour alternately with wine. Shape into small balls between the palms. Flatten each cookie with the bottom of a small glass dipped in sugar and cinnamon. Bake at 375 for bout 10 minutes and sprinkle while hot with more cinnamon and sugar; heavy on the cinnamon, if you wish.

Portuguese Walnut Squares (Bert's)

½ c softened butter (not runny or whipped)	Port
¾ c packed light-brown sugar	8 T all purpose flour
1 egg	½ t baking powder
½ t vanilla	walnuts
2 T milk	Glaze

Cream butter and sugar. Add egg and beat well. Add vanilla, milk and 2 T port. Grind or grate 1 cup walnuts. Place in mixing bowl. Add dry ingredients and stir. Fold in butter egg mixture to make a batter. Do not over beat. Spoon into lightly buttered and floured 9" sq. cake pan. Bake in 350 oven for 20 – 30 minutes until cake tests just done. Remove from oven and at once brush top with 2 to 3 T Port. Cool to room temperature and spread with glaze.

Glaze : 1 cup confectioners sugar, dash of salt
      1 T softened butter
      1 T port or enough to make glaze of spreading consistency.

Mix above ingredients well. Tint a light pink with a little red food coloring. Spread on cooled cake and sprinkle with chopped walnuts. Let stand until firm. Cut into 16 squares.

Note: Madeira can be substituted for port, it desired.

Squares will remain fresh at least 3 weeks at room temperature if stored airtight.

Sweet Potato Pie

Rich pastry for a one crust nine inch pie.

1- ½ lbs. sweet potatoes	1 – ½ T brandy
¼ lb. sweet butter, melted	½ t nutmeg
2/3 c superfine sugar	1 – ½ t cinnamon
3 eggs slightly beaten	Pinch salt

Line 9 inch pie plate with pastry and crimp the edges. Then refrigerate. Wash and peel potatoes, cut in quarters, cover with water and cook until tender (about 20 min.) Drain well and mash. Stir in the butter, sugar, then the eggs, brandy and spices. Push through a sieve and fill the pastry shell. Bake in the preheated 400 oven until filling tests done when pierced with sharp knife – 35 to 40 min. Cool on a cake rack. Do not refrigerate. To boil sweet potatoes: Cover with boiling salted water, cover and cook quickly until tender. If peeled before cooking, cover with salted water to keep from turning dark.

Orange Waldorf Salad

2 med unpared apples diced (2 cups)
1 T lemon juice
1 cup diced celery
3 med oranges, sectioned
¼ cup chopped walnuts
½ cup mayonnaise thinned or salad dressing

Sprinkle apple with lemon juice. In a salad bowl combine apple, celery, orange sections, walnuts and mayonnaise. Toss together. Chill till served. 6 Servings.

Avocado Shrimp salad

2 T lemon juice	1 cup cleaned cooked shrimp
¼ t salt	3 hard cooked eggs
¼ cup mayonnaise	1 tomato
½ cup diced celery	avocado

Have all ingredients chilled. Add lemon juice and salt to mayonnaise. Dice avocado and toss in the dressing. Cut shrimp and add with eggs, peeled, drained chopped tomato and celery. Toss lightly and serve on lettuce leaves with a sprinkle of paprika and a spring of parsley. Serves 4

Three Bean salad Bowl

1 pkg frozen cut green beans	2/3 cup vinegar
1 pkg frozen cut wax beans	½ cup sugar
1 can (1 lb.) red kidney beans drained	½ cup salad oil
1 green pepper slivered (1 cup)	1 clove garlic, split
½ cup thinly sliced red onion	1 t salt and 1/8 t pepper
	½ t Wooster sauce

Cook green and wax beans as pkg labels direct. Drain; let cool. In large salad bowl combine cooled beans, kidney beans, green pepper and onion. In jar with tight fitting lid, combine vinegar, sugar, salad oil, garlic, salt, Wooster and pepper; shake vigorously. Discard garlic. Pour over bean mixture; toss until well combined. Good for buffet.

Cooked Veggie Salad

In separate saucepans cook 2 carrots, 2 potatoes, ¼ lb. green beans, and 1 cup chilled peas in boiling salted water until each vegetable is just tender. Drain the veggies, let them cool and peel the potatoes. Dice the carrots, potatoes and green beans and put them in a bowl with the peas. Add on cucumber, peeled, seeded and diced, two stalks of celery diced, and 1/3 cup minced onion; Chill the mixture for two hours. In another bowl combine ½ cup each of mayonnaise and sour cream, 1 T lemon juice and salt and white pepper to taste. Toss the veggies lightly with the dressing. Serves 4-6.

Pickled Beets and Eggs

2 cans (1 lb. size) small whole beets	1/8 t ground cloves
1 cup cider vinegar	1 med onion sliced
½ c sugar	12 hard cooked eggs
1 t salt	

Drain the beets, reserve one cup juice. In medium saucepan combine vinegar, sugar, salt, cloves, onion and reserved beet juice. Bring to boil stirring occasionally. Add beets; simmer uncovered 10 minutes. Shell eggs and place in a half gallon jar. Slowly pour in beets and liquid. Stir gently to distribute eggs evenly through the beets. Let cool; then refrigerate, covered until well chilled at least 24 hours. Makes 12 servings.

WARM THE PLATES

Dilled Veal Special

2 lbs. ground veal
8 slices bacon, crisp-cooked, drained and crumpled

½ cup fine dry bread crumbs	2 chicken bouillon cubes
½ cup milk	3 cups boiling water
2 beaten eggs	1 t kitchen bouquet
1 t salt	2 T water
½ t dill weed	2 T cornstarch

Combine veal, crumbled bacon, bread crumbs, milk, eggs, salt and dill weed; mix thoroughly. Shape into 36 meatballs. Dissolved bouillon cubes in the 3 cups of boiling water and add kitchen bouquet. Pour into a large skillet. Add meatballs and bring to boiling. Cook, covered for 30 minutes; turn veal once during cooking. Transfer veal balls to serving dish. Blend the cornstarch and water; stir into broth in skillet and cook over low heat for a couple minutes till thickened. Pour sauce over veal balls; serve with hot cooked rice or noodles. Makes 8 servings.

Zucchini with Tomatoes

1 green zucchini and 1 yellow zucchini
8 cherry tomatoes
1 med onion fried in 2-3 T butter

Wash veggies thoroughly. Cut them length wise in halves and then in ¼" slices. Fry onion in the butter until limp. Add the zuks, mix gently, add salt and pepper and cover pan. Simmer for 10-15 minutes, stirring once. Then add the halved cherry tomatoes, a scant tsp sugar, cover pan and cook over low heat for bout 15 minutes. Take a look at it now and then and stir it a bit. That does it. It's a cheap, colorful summer dish, different and tasty.

Raisin Nut Fold Overs

1 can (ten biscuits) refrigerater Buttermilk biscuits
¾ cup white raisins
1/3 cup chopped nuts
2 T butter
3 T sugar
½ t cinnamon
1 egg beaten

Heat over to 400. Lightly grease cookie sheet. Separate biscuit dough into ten biscuits. Press or roll each to a 5-6" circle. Combine raisins, nuts, butter, sugar and cinnamon. Spoon about one T raisin mixture onto center of each biscuit. Fold biscuit over filling. Press edges with fork. Place on cookie sheet. Brush with egg. Bake at 400 for 10-12 minutes or until golden brown. Serve warm. Raisin-nut mixture can be made in advance.

Honey Ham Loaf (A & P)

Mix ¼ cup honey, ¾ cup crushed pineapple, 1/8 t cloves. Spread in buttered loaf pan. Combine 1 cup bread crumbs, one lb. ground uncooked ham, one lb. uncooked pork; 2 eggs, ¼ t pepper, 1 T prepared mustard salt to taste and 1 – ¼ cups milk. Pack mixture in pan. Bake at 350 for 1- ¼ hours. Turn out with fruit on top. Serve with quick-cooked cabbage, baked yams, biscuits and applesauce.

Bacon Popovers

In large bowl combine 1 cup sifted flour with ½ t salt, 3 eggs lightly beaten, 1 cup milk and 2 T melted butter. Beat the batter with a rotary beater until it is smooth. Stir in ½ cup cooked and crumbled bacon. Butter iron popover pans and heat them until they are sizzling hot. Fill the cups half full with batter and bake in a very hot 450 oven for 20 mins. Reduce temperature to 350 and bake for about 20 minutes more, or until they are brown and crisp.

Pie crust ala blue ribbon winner:

> 1 c lard
> 3 c flour
> 1 egg
> 1 T vinegar and 1 t salt

Always cook the pie fillings before adding to the raw pie shell. They bake better and faster and the crust doesn't get too brown. Tear strips of aluminum foil and crease them all around the edges of the crusts so the crusts don't brown too fast.

Gooseberry Pie

2/3 c water, divided	¼ c cornstarch
2 c sugar	1 T butter
1 qt gooseberries	two crust unbaked pie shell

Cook 1/3 c water and the sugar for 2-3 minutes. Add berries and simmer gently for 5 minutes; strain berries from syrup. Dissolve cornstarch in 1/3 c cold water; add butter, then berries. Place berry mixture in pie shell; place top crust on pie. Bake at 425 for 15 minutes; reduce heat to 350 and cook for 30 minutes more or until done.

Cherry Pie

1 quart frozen cherries	1 T butter
1 – ½ c sugar	¼ t almond extract
1 T and 1 t tapioca	¼ t red food coloring
2 T cornstarch	¼ t salt
¾ c reserved cherry juice	two crust unbaked pie shell

Drain defrosted cherries; reserve juice. Combine sugar, tapioca, cornstarch and juice; cook until thick. Add butter, almond extract coloring and salt. Stir in drained cherries and pour into pie shell; add top crust. Bake at 425 for 10 minutes reduce heat to 375 and bake for 30 minutes more or until pie is bubbly and brown

Honey yeast bread

2 t salt	1 pkg dry yeast
¼ c butter	¼ c warm water
¼ c honey	6 – ½ to 7 cups flour
2 – ½ c scalded milk	

Melt salt, butter and honey in scalded milk; let cool to lukewarm. Dissolve yeast in warm water. Add 2 cups flour to cooled milk; mix well. Add dissolved yeast and rest of flour. Turn out onto floured board; knead until dough is not sticky. Place in greased bowl; let rise 1 – ½ to 2 hours or until double in size. Punch dough down, divide and shape into two loaves. Place in greased 8 x 4 x 2 inch loaf pans. Let dough rise about 45 minutes. Bake at 350 for 45 minutes. Remove from pans; cool on wire racks.

Lemon Angels

Mix Betty Crocker one-step angel food cake with one can of lemon pudding by hand. Spread on well greased cookie sheet and bake for 20 minutes at 350. Allow to cool and cute into finger size pieces. Sprinkle with XXX sugar.

Camille's Nutty Crunchy Sweet Potato Pie

Makes one 9" pie
Ingredients:

½ cup sugar	2 eggs
1 tsp cinnamon	1 cup of milk
½ tsp nutmeg	2 T butter
¼ tsp salt	1 cup chopped English walnuts
1 ½ cups mashed sweet potatoes (canned or fresh)	1,9" unbaked pie shell

Preparation:
1. Mix together sugar, cinnamon, nutmeg and salt.
2. Stir in sweet potatoes
3. Combine eggs, milk, walnuts and butter
4. Pour into pie shell
Bake in a hot 400 oven for approximately 40 minutes or until center of pie is set

Date Bars

¼ cup melted butter   ¼ t baking powder
1 cup sugar   few grains salt
2 eggs well beaten   1 cup dates cut fine
¾ cup flour   1 cup chopped nuts

Mix in order given. Spread in pan lined with waxed paper. Bake 15 to 20 minutes in 350 oven. Cut in finger-shaped pieces (while warm) and roll in powdered sugar.

Ice Cream Soda

In tall glasses combine 3 heaping t of powdered chocolate mix and 1 t instant coffee with small amount of milk. Mix thoroughly. Add one scoop of ice cream, now fill slowly with chilled club soda.

Orange Frosties:

8 sandwich-size plastic bags
1 pint vanilla ice cream, softened
2 cups orange juice
4 large sturdy straws, cut in half

Place sandwich bags, open side up in cups, mugs, empty 8 oz vegetable cans or similar holder; set aside. With whisk beat ice cream and orange juice until well blended and smooth. Pour ½ cup mixture into each bag. Insert straw; fasten bag with twist tie. Freeze. Let stand 10 to 15 minutes at room temperature before serving. Sip mixture from bag as it melts. Makes 8 servings.

You can do this with frozen grape juice too.

Banana Milkshake – one med-large banana, one cup milk

Peel banana, wrap in foil and freeze. Cut frozen banana into chunks. Place milk and one T sugar in blender. Gradually add banana, blending on medium speed till smooth. Makes two servings.

Miscellaneous

Salmon or tuna puffs (heloise)

14 oz canned salmon or tuna
one egg
one half cup flour
one heaping teaspoon baking powder.

Drain the salmon or tuna, reserving one fourth cup liquid. Put the meat into a mixing bowl, break apart well with a fork, then add the flour and slightly beaten egg. Add pepper if desired. Mix well.

Add the baking powder to the reserved liquid, then beat well with a fork until foamy. Pout this into the salmon mixture, then stir until blended.using two teaspoons, scoop the mixture out with one spoon and with another place the mixture into a deep fryer, half full of hot corn oil.
Don't worry about the shapes- your family won't. The little tidbits are done practically instantly, so keep an eye on them, removing from the oil as soon as they are brown. Drain on paper towels, serve and enjoy.

Ice cream drinks

"Alexander icicle"
2 T crème decacao
 2 T brandy
1 pint coffee ice cream
sweetened whipped cream, for garnish or candy coffee beans for garnish

Combine crème de cacao, brandy and ice cream in blender. Cover and whirl until smooth and foamy. Pour into serving glasses. If desired garnish each with a spoon of whipped cream and a coffee bean. Serve immediately.

Jimmy salmon patties

1 can (15 oz) salmon
½ c chopped green onions
¼ c chopped parsley
1 c fine dry bread crumbs

2 beaten eggs
1 t prepared mustard
2 T lemon juice
2 T corn oil

Drain and flake salmon, reserving 1/3 c liquid. Combine salmon with green onions parsley and bread crumbs. Add beaten eggs, mustard, lemon juice and reserved salmon liquid. Shape into patties and fry in oil over medium heat until lightly browned on both sides. Makes 6 servings.

Rancho deviled crab

2 T butter
2 T chopped onion
2 T chopped green pepper
½ c thinly slice celery
3 T melted butter
½ c soft bread crumbs

2 T flour
¼ t dry mustard
½ t salt
1 c milk

½ t Worchester sauce
½ c diced pimiento
1 c flaked crab(8 oz)
½ c chopped ripe olives

Melt butter over low heat; add onion, green pepper and celery and cook until veggies are tender but not browned. Add flour, mustard and salt. Blend until smooth. Gradually stir in milk and cook, stirring until thickened. Blend in Worchester sauce, pimiento, crab meat and olives. Turn into ramekins or baking shells. Toss bread crumbs into melted butter. Spoon buttered crumbs evenly over top of crab mixture. Bake in hot oven 400 about 15 min. serves 3

Tuna fish salad (niesse's)

¼ cup diced celery
1 can tuna
1cup tiny peas
1 hard cooked egg

2 T chopped pickle
mayonnaise

Flake tuna with fork, add peas, chopped egg, celery and pickle. Marinate the ingredients with desired amount of mayonnaise ad serve in lettuce nest. Serves 4.

Dumplings

2 lbs. flour
2eggs

½ pt ice water
¼ lb butter

Mix ingredients, roll out on floured board. Then slice diagonally into diamond shapes. Allow to rest about half hr. Drop into hot chicken broth. Very delicious. Serves 10.

Chicken aspic

Whole chicken
2 pkgs gelatin
½ cup cold water

½ cup chopped celery
¼ cup chopped green pepper
½ t salt if needed

Simmer whole chicken in salted water until tender(1-2 hrs.) Cool. Bone chicken and cut into small pieces. (or use already cooked and boned chicken). To four cups of hot chicken broth add the gelatin and finely chopped celery and pepper. Pour over chicken in mold and chill to set. Serve on lettuce with mayonnaise thinned with cream. Garnish with finely chopped olives.

Chicken pie

Prepare one medium sized chicken for stew. Make about three cups of gravy as the crust will soak up quite a bit of it. Place the cut up chicken in a baking dish, add the gravy and pour the following batter over it:

Batter: 2 cups flour   7/8 cup milk
1 ½ t salt   2 T cooking oil
2t baking powder   2 well beaten eggs

Sift flour, salt and baking powder, combine other ingredients and add to the sifted flour mixture, stirring the batter as little as possible. Pour over chicken and bake in 375 oven until lightly browned. Serves 6.

Chicken salad (niesse's)

1 ½ cups cubed cooked chicken   ¼ t salt
2 T French dressing   pepper
1 cup chopped celery   mayonnaise
1 chopped hard cooked egg   lettuce
½ chopped blanched almonds

Marinate chicken in french dressing; let stand awhile, then drain. Combine ingredients and add mayonnaise. This salad may be molded in individual molds, or into a ring. Moisten the molds with water first. Pack solid and chill until firm and turn out on lettuce leaf, top with a dab of mayonnaise.

Baked macaroni and cheese

Two cups cooked macaroni	¾ t salt
4t minced onion	dash pepper
2 T butter	2 cups milk
1 T flour	½ lbs. cheddar
¼ t dry mustard	¼ c shredded cheddar
¾ cup soft bread crumbs	4 t melted butter

In top of double boiler put minced onion, 2 T butter, stir well and add flour, mustard, salt, pepper and blend. Add milk, cook until smooth stirring often. Grate ½ lb. cheddar and add ¾ of it to the sauce stirring constantly until cheese melts. Turn the macaroni into a greased casserole and pour over it the cheese sauce while tossing it lightly so all the macaroni is coated with cheese. Sprinkle the rest of the cheese over the top; also ¾ cup fine soft bread crumbs which have been tossed in 4 t melted butter.bake 20-25 min in a 400 oven. Serves 6

Baked cream fish fillets

2 lbs fish fillets (halibut)	2 T flour
¼ t salt, dash pepper	juice of one lemon
¼ t paprika	1 T dry mustard
1 cup cream	2 T flour
½ cup buttered crumbs	1 T minced parsley

Cut fillets into serving pieces. Place in greased shallow baking dish, sprinkle with s&p, paprika and lemon juice. Make white sauce of butter, flour, seasonings and cream (1/2 &1/2) pour over fillets. Sprinkle with crumbs and parsley. Bake in 350 oven about 35 min. serves 4.

Baked oysters

1 qt large oysters

1 egg

1 T water

¾ cup dry bread crumbs

1/3 t onion juice

3 T chopped celery

2 T butter

½ cup cream

s&p

Beat egg with water, dip oysters in egg, then in crumbs, put in baking dish in layers and sprinkle celery and seasonings. Spread with bread crumbs. Dot with butter, add cream. Bake in hot oven 30 min.

Salmon puffs

2 cups salmon

1 T melted butter

½ cup bread crumbs

1 T lemon juice

3 well beaten eggs

s&p

parsley to garnish

2 egg whites, beaten till stiff

Flake salmon and add lemon juice; combine crumbs, melted butter and seasonings, then mix with salmon. Add well beaten eggs, mix thoroughly. Fold in egg whites. Pack into greased custard cups, filling about ¾ full. Set cups in pan of hot water and bake in moderate oven (350) for ½ hr. Turn puffs out on platter, garnish with parsley and pour salmon sauce around them.

Salmon sauce:

1 cup hot milk

1 T lemon juice

2 well beaten egg yolks   s&p

Slowly pour the hot milk over the well beaten egg yolks. Set in bowl of hot water and stir until thick, taking care mixture does not overheat. When thick, add lemon juice and s&p to taste. Serves 4-6.

Party chicken salad

3 cups cooked chicken, 1 ½ c diced celery. 3 T lemon juice, 1 cup seedless grapes, 1 cup toasted almonds, 1 t dry mustard, 1 ½ t salt, pepper, ¼ cup light cream, 1 cup mayonnaise.

Combine chicken, celery and lemon juice and chill for 1 hour. Add grapes and almonds. Combine remaining ingredients and add to chicken. Toss. Garnish with slices of hardcooked egg. Serves 6.

Speedy picked peaches

One 29-ounce can peach halves
Whole cloves
½ cup vinegar
½ cup sugar
3 inches stick cinnamon, broken

Drain peaches, reserving one cup syrup. Stud each peach half with 3 or 4 cloves. Combine reserved syrup, vinegar, sugar and cinnamon. Add peaches. Bring o boiling; simmer uncovered 3 to 4 minutes. Cool. Cover; refrigerate. Before using, drain peaches and remove cinnamon. Serve with meat, fish or poultry.

Brandied peaches

2 cups sugar
about 2" stick cinnamon
2 cups water
6-8 small fresh peaches (2 lbs.peeled)
brandy

Combine sugar, water and cinnamon. Bring to a boil. Boil rapidly five min. Add a few whole peaches at a time and cook 5-10 minutes or until peaches can be easily pierced with a fork. Remove fruit from syrup; pack in hot scalded jars. Boil remaining syrup till thickened. Cool syrup to room temperature. Measure syrup. Add 1/3 cup brandy for each cup syrup. Stir well; fill jars with brandy syrup. Seal jars at once. Makes 3-4 pints.

Calico bean salad

1 can (1lb) del Monte cut green beans, drained
1 jar (lb) del Monte sliced carrots, drained
1 can (12 oz) del Monte whole kernel corn
2 T chopped onion
celery seed dressing
salad greens

Combine vegetables. Toss with celery seed dressing. Chill in covered container several hours or overnight. Serve on salad greens; 6-8 servings.

Celery seed dressing:
½ c brown sugar
1/3 cup cider vinegar
1 T salt, 2t celery seed
¼ t tumeric, dash pepper
Combine all ingredients.

Holiday green bean casserole

2 cans (lb each) cut green beans drained or
2 pkgs (9ozs each) frozen cut green beans, cooked and drained
¾ cup milk
1 can condensed cream/mushroom soup
1/8 t pepper
1 can (2.8 oz) Durkee Fr. Fried Onions

Combine beans, milk, soup, pepper and ½ can of French fried onions. Pour into a 1 ½ qt casserole. Bake uncovered at 350 for 30 mins. Top with remaining onions and bake 5 mins. longer. 6 Servings.

Hillbillies

Six med. sweet potatoes. Peeled   1 bunch watercress for garnish or parsley
½ cup brown sugar
12 slices bacon

Boil potatoes until tender; cut in half lengthwise. Wrap each half in one slice bacon and fasten with a toothpick. Heat frying pan, put in potatoes, sprinkle with sugar. Turn as soon as bacon begins to frizzle. Brown on other side. Serves 6 to 12. Good for buffet.

Blackeyed peas and rice (hoppin john)

1 lb dried black-eyed peas, washed & picked over
1-2 ham hocks (at least one lb)
½ cup chopped onion (1 medium)
salt and pepper (watch it the ham hocks may be salty enough)
dash cayenne
1 cup uncooked long grain rice (I recommend uncle Ben's)

Soak peas overnite in three cups water. Drain. Measure water and add enough to make three cups. In large heavy saucepan bring soaked peas, water, ham hocks onion and bit of salt to boil. Cover and simmer 1-1/2 hours or until peas are tender and only a small amount of liquid remains. Remove meat from bones if desired. Add to peas with black and red peppers. Cook rice according to package directions. Add a bit of butter and mix lightly with peas and ham meat. Makes 6-8 servings.

Chicken and rice

In ungreased pan put 2 cups uncooked rice. Lay two cut up chickens, skin side up, on top of dry rice. Mix together one cup cream of mushroom soup and two cans orange juice (*no kidding*). Pour over chicken and rice. Sprinkle one envelope liptons' onion soup mix over top. Cover with foil and bake 2-1/2 hrs. at 325. Serves 6-8.

Mushroom chowder

Combine condensed cream of mushroom soup with one can of light cream, one can of lightly sautéed sliced mushrooms, a few T of lightly sautéed onion and sieved hard boiled eggs. Heat and serve. *It's good!* Serves 4.

Rum sauce

In saucepan combine 1 cup cold water and 2 T cornstarch. Add ¼ cup sugar and cook mixture until it is thickened. Remove the pan from heat and add one cup each dark rum and orange juice. Cook the sauce over moderate heat, stirring, for 5 mins. Pour over pound cake.

Chocolate walnut dollars (bert's)

2-1/2 cups cake flour sifted	½ t cinnamon
1 t baking powder	1 cup sugar
1 egg slightly beaten	½ cup soft butter
2 T milk	2sqs baker's unsweetened chocolate, melted.
½ cup cup walnut meats, chopped	1 t vanilla

Sift flour once, measure, add baking powder and cinnamon and sift together three times. Combine remaining ingredients then add flour, mixing well. Shape in 2" roll, wrap in waxed paper; chill thoroughly. Cut in 1/8" slices. Bake on greased sheet in hot oven 400 for 5 minutes. Makes a lot.

Tomatoes stuffed with cucumbers

Cut top quarter from six ripe med. tomatoes which have been peeled. Scoop out the pulp and sprinkle shells lightly with salt and pepper. Invert tomatoes on a rack, let them drain for 30 minutes. Peel and seed two cukes and cut them into ½ inch cubes. In a bowl combine ½ cup sour cream, 1 t Worchester, ½ t salt and ¼ t lemon juice and pepper to taste and stir in the cukes. Fill the tomato cases with the cuke mixture and sprinkle with chopped dill.

Tuna salad (lena's)

2 c tuna   1 c mayonnaise
2c grated carrots   2 T French dressing
1 cup chopped celery 2 T sugar
1 T onion

Let salad set 3 hrs. Fold in can of shoestring potatoes before serving.

Shrimp and seashells

Add cream of mushroom soup and a lump of butter to cooked seashells and shrimps. Parsley to garnish.

Baked pork chops, whipped potatoes, buttered new cabbage, green salad

Chops 1- 1/2 thick

Put in baking pan, salt and pepper, put a slice of lemon and t brown sugar on each. Then half ketchup and half water and pour on chops so they're just covered. Bake one hr. in medium oven.

Salad- orange and onion slices

Orange, onion and olive salad- arrange thin slices of Bermuda or other mild onion and orange slices on watercress. Garnish with sliced black olives and serve with French dressing.

Avocado sandwiches

Trim crusts from thinly sliced white bread. Spread them with butter and salt and pepper. Slice peeled avocado thinly and marinate in lemon juice for one hour. Drain slices and sandwich them between buttered bread. Cut into four triangles and chill before serving.

Cucumber sandwiches

Cut thin sliced white bread with round biscuit cutter. Butter one round and spread with mayonnaise on other round. Marinate cucumber slices in vinegar/water, salt and pepper and sugar for one jour. Drain slices and sandwich them between the buttered/mayonnaise bread. Wrap in wax paper and chill before serving.

Quick apple strudels

2 small apples, peeled, cored and thinly sliced
lemon juice
¼ t cinnamon   1 pkg (8) refrigerated crescent rolls
½ c raisins (white)   sifted xxx sugar
½ c packed brown sugar

Preheat oven to 400. Dip apple slices in lemon juice. In bowl combine raisins, brown sugar, and cinnamon. Unroll crescent dough and separate into four rectangles. Pinch together seam in each rectangle. Place rectangles of dough on baking sheet. Sprinkle with raisin mixture. Place apple slices side by side on narrow end of dough rectangle. Roll up as for a jelly roll, ending seam side down. Pinch ends to seal. Bake in 400 oven 15 min. remove to wire rack; cool 10 mins. Sprinkle with xxx sugar. Makes 4

Islander chicken

No. 2 can pineapple chunks drained   ¼ cup chopped onion
Reserve syrup   ¼ cup soy sauce
1 can condensed chicken broth   3 T cornstarch
1 pkg frozen peas   3 T water
1 can (4oz) sliced mushrooms, drained   4 cups diced cooked chicken

1 ½ cups celery cut in 1" diagonal slices   1 can (5oz) water chestnuts, drained and sliced in a large saucepan, combine pineapple, syrup, broth, peas, mushrooms, celery, onion and soy sauce. Bring to boil; simmer uncooked 5 minutes. Combine cornstarch and water; stir into saucepan mixture; cook, stirring, until thickened. Stir in remaining ingredients. Heat thoroughly, serve over Chinese noodles.

Cranberry nut bread

2 cups flour	1 T grated orange peel
1 cup sugar	2 T shortening
1 ½ t baking powder	1 well beaten egg
1 t salt	1 ½ cups fresh or frozen cranberries coarsely chopped
½ t baking soda	½ cup chopped nuts
¾ cup orange juice	

Preheat oven to 350. In a bowl mix together flour, sugar, baking powder, salt and baking soda. Stir in orange juice, orange peel, shortening and egg. Mix until well blended. Stir in cranberries and nuts. Turn into a greased 9 x 5 loaf pan. Bake 55 min. or until toothpick inserted in center comes out clean. Cool on a rack 15 min. Remove from pan. Makes one loaf.

Dilled new potatoes, dill pickles and buttermilk. (lunch)

Scrape small new red potatoes. Cook them with 1 t salt and 1 t caraway until done-approx. 20 mins. Make cream sauce and add ½ cup sour cream with 1T lemon juice and 1 T chopped fresh dill to sauce. Put cooked potatoes into this. Serve this hot or cold with a crunchy dill pickle (not a brine one) and a glass of buttermilk. Very refreshing and summery.

Creamed celery

2 Tbutter
2 cups center celery stalks cut into 2-3" pieces
1 can chicken broth (or your own soup)

Sauté celery in butter about 2-3 min. pour on broth and simmer about 10 minutes. Thicken with flour and milk.

Little Yummies

Pear waldorf salad -like traditional except pears instead of apples.

Peach with cottage cheese salad. Fill canned peach halves with c.c. and a bit of fr. Dressing.

Tomato, grapefruit and cuke salad.

Clear tomato soup served with salted whipped cream.

Celery, grapes, banana, apples, lettuce with mayonnaise.

Vanilla ice cream with Gran Marnier.

Anchovy dressing – ½ cup Italian dressing mixed with 2 t finely cut anchovies, Serve over tossed greens, cherry toms, green pepper and mushrooms.

Pineapple rice Bavarian

1 cup canned pureed pineapple (blender)
2 cups sugar syrup (1 c sugar, 1 c water)
2 cups cooked rice (use mushy rice)
juice of 1 lemon

1- ½ oz. gelatin
2 cups whipped cream
8 pineapple slices, fresh if possible

Mix fruit puree with sugar syrup and cooked rice. Add lemon juice, dissolved and strained gelatin and whipped cream. Mix well and pour in mold well oiled with sweet almond oil. Chill till set. Turn out and arrange pineapple around rice. Serves 4.

Coeur a la crème

1 lb cream cheese
¼ cup cream
¼ t salt
2 T powdered sugar

This is one of the most pleasant of cheese desserts. Mix the cream cheese with the cream, salt and sugar. Line a heart-shaped mold with wet cheese cloth, pour in the cheese mixture and chill. Turn out on a dish, surround with strawberry preserves and serve with butter biscuits. Serves about 6.

Delicate spice cake

1 stick butter	2 t cinnamon
2 cups dark brown sugar, packed	2 t ginger
3 eggs	½ t nutmeg
2 ¼ cups sifted flour	¼ t ground cloves
¼ t salt	1 cup sour cream
1 t baking soda	

Cream butter, gradually adding the brown sugar. Add one egg at a time, beating well after each addition. Preheat oven to 350. sift together flour, salt, baking powder, cinnamon, ginger, nutmeg and cloves. Add to the butter mixture alternately with the sour cream. Divide between two buttered 8 inch layer cake pans. Bake 30 mins or until a cake tester comes out clean. Cool on cake rack and ice with the following:

¼ cup melted butter
2 cups xxx sugar
¾ cup heavy cream

Mix the butter and sugar together. Add just enough cream to make the mixture spread able. Ice the cake when it has completely cooled.

Nut and honey cake

2 eggs	1 T salad oil
½ cup sugar	2 cups sifted cake flour
¼ cup brewed coffee	1/8 t salt
1 cup honey	¾ t baking powder
½ t baking soda	
1 cup shelled filberts	2 T cognac

Oil a 10 inch loaf pan and line it with waxed paper or aluminum foil. Preheat the oven to 325. Beat the eggs; gradually add the sugar. Beat until light and fluffy. Add the coffee, honey and oil, mixing well. Sift together flour, salt, baking powder, and baking soda; add the nuts. Add gradually to the honey mixture stirring steadily. Add the cognac. Pour into pan. Bake 55 min or until cake tester comes out clean. Cool in pan or on a cake rack. This is a moist cake and will keep well.

Chilled creamy tomato soup

One 46 oz can Hunts tomato juice, chilled
1 ½ t salt
½ t basil
1 ½ cups sour cream
2 T chopped chives

Mix all ingredients except chives. Blend with beater or by hand. Sprinkle with chives. Serve in chilled glass bowls if possible (*pretty*). Serve small tuna salad, chicken salad or cucumber sandwiches with it. 6-8 servings.

Mighty mousse

1 can tomato soup (campbells)
½ cup sour cream
1 t lemon juice
2 envs. unflavored gelatin
2 cups cut chicken- baked or boiled
¾ cup chopped cucumber
½ cup sliced stuffed olives
 2 T minced onion

In bowl, gradually blend soup into sour cream; add lemon juice, ½ t salt and pepper. Soften gelatin in one soup can water. Stir over low heat until gelatin is dissolved. Remove from heat; blend with soup mixture. Chill until slightly thickened; fold in remaining ingredients. Pour into five cup mold. Chill your mighty mousse for 4 hrs. Makes 4 servings.

Chicken a la king

¼ lb butter. Melt slowly in double boiler; blend in ½ cup flour and 1 ½ t salt. Little by little add one cup each milk, cream, and chicken stock. When thoroughly cooked, add one lb. chicken breast and thighs cut into large cubes, ¼ lb sliced and sautéed mushrooms, 3 T pimiento, ½ cup green pepper (cooked in chicken stock). Just before serving, add ½ c sherry. Serve on toast, noodles, in pastry shells, rice etc. add color- green vegetables and spiced peach, grilled tomato, kumquat, baked peach or pear filled with jelly, grenadine grapefruit slices, sautéed pineapple ring, etc., etc. Serves 6.

Cornish hens with Pecan Stuffing

Rub with melted butter. Roast in preheated oven at 400 for one hour, basting every 20 minutes with pan drippings. If you stuff the hens, add half hour roasting time.

Pecan stuffing:

1 med onion, chopped
1/3 cup chopped celery
½ cup butter
1 t salt

1 ½ cups chopped pecans
½ cup chopped parsley
5 slices bread, diced

Grapefruit shrimp salad

4 grapefruit
2 (4 ½ oz each) cans shrimp, drained in cold water
1 cup chopped celery
1/3 to ½ cup mayonnaise diluted with milk/cream

Cut grapefruit in halves. With a grapefruit knife, cut around each segment and remove; place segments in a small bowl. Carefully remove and discard membranes from four grapefruit shells, keeping shells intact. Discard remaining shells. Drain grapefruit segments well; add shrimp and celery, stir in enough of the mayonnaise to moisten. To serve, spoon into the 4 grapefruit shells. Makes 4 servings. Serve with hot rolls, and cake for dessert.

Pork goulash

3 T butter
2 onions
1 t caraway
1 clove garlic
1 T dill, salt and pepper
2 ½ lb pork shoulder
½ c water
1 T paprika
1 lb sauerkraut
½ c sour cream

Melt butter and stir in sliced onions, meat and salt, pepper, caraway, garlic. "Grey" this mixture. Add paprika water and sauerkraut after 3 min. Cover and cook over low heat for about one hour. Stir in sour cream. Serve with boiled potatoes.

Sherry tarts

1/3 c sugar
3 T sherry or 2 T rum
1/8 t salt
2 eggs
2 c cream

½ c milk
8 tart shells, med size
1 t sugar
grated nutmeg

Mix dry ingredients. Add eggs, slightly beaten. Blend thoroughly. Reserve ½ c cream. Scald rest of cream and milk. Then pour it gradually over egg mixture, stirring constantly. Cook about 15 mins in top of double- boiler, continuing so flour will not lump. Cool, add sherry or rum. Whip reserved cream with 1 t of sugar until it is thick but not quite stiff. Fill shells with custard, top with cream and grate a dash of nutmeg over each.

Old time sponge cake

8 eggs   2 c flour (sifted)

2 c sugar   1 ½ t vinegar

1 dessertspoon vanilla

Separate eggs and beat in different bowls, adding one cup of sugar to each mixture. Put together and add the vinegar and sifted flour. Add vanilla and bake in slow oven 250 for 30 min and in quicker oven for 30 min. longer in an angel food cake pan.

Sweet pickled watermelon

1 watermelon rind   4 T whole cloves

4 c vinegar   2 T cinnamon sticks

8 lbs. sugar

Cut skin from watermelon; cut rind into small pieces about 2 inches square. After cutting melon, soak in 1 cup salt and enough water to cover for 12 to 13 hrs. then pour off and boil in fresh water. Boil sugar and vinegar 10 min. Add spices ties in bag. Simmer until syrupy, about 2 hours. Add melon and simmer one hour. Fill jars and seal. Yield: 12 pints

Molded salad

1pkg lemon gelatine   ½ c chopped nuts

1 T vinegar   1 c chopped cucumber

1 c hot water   1 c celery (diced fine)

Dissolve gelatin in hot water. Add vinegar. Allow to cool and then add nuts, cuke and celery. Mold. Serves 8.

Bing cherry mold

One 2 lb. can bing cherries (2 ½ c)   1 c port wine
1 pkg cherry gelatine   1 envelope gelatine
1(3oz) pkg cream cheese

Heat one cup cherry juice and the port. Pour remaining cherry juice over plain gelatine. Put both gelatines together and dissolve in the hot cherry juice and port. Stir and mix together. Add cherries that have been cut in half and pitted. Put in ring mold. Serve with cream cheese that has been softened with cream.

Pineapple fritters

1 egg   1c crushed and drained pineapple
1 c milk (scant)   2 T butter melted
3 T sugar   2 ½ c flour to make stiff batter
2 ½ t baking powder

Combine in order given. Add pineapple to batter last. Drop a tablespoonful at a time in hot deep fat. Serve with sauce.

Sauce for pineapple fritters

1c brown sugar   1 c water
2 T flour   1 c pineapple juice
½ lemon juice   2 t butter

Combine and cook until clear.

Pistachio ice cream

4 c light cream   ¼ t salt
1 c sugar   ½ c pistachio nuts
1 T almond extract   1 c almonds
green coloring

Chop pistachios and almonds fine. Whip cream, then add other ingredients and nuts. Color with delicate green coloring, freeze.

Sherry sauce for vanilla ice cream

½ c milk   1 c sugar

2 T sherry   4 T butter

Boil milk, sugar and butter together for five minutes. Add sherry.

Sweet potato pie

3 large potatoes   ½ t nutmeg

2 T butter   2 egg whites

½ c sugar   1 egg

½ t cinnamon   4 t sugar

Boil potatoes until soft. Peel and mash well with 2 t butter. Add sugar cinnamon, nutmeg and egg, well beaten. Fill cooked pastry shell and cover with meringue made of beaten egg whites and 4 T sugar. Brown in med. 350° oven. Serves 6

Junk food

Graham cracker cookies (liz)

Line cookie sheet with aluminum foil. Lay graham crackers on it. Cook two sticks butter and on cup brown sugar for two minutes; spread over graham crackers with back of spoon. Bake 6 minutes in 400 oven. Then sprinkle 12 oz chocolate chips (or butterscotch) over hot graham crackers. These will melt; again spread over hot graham crackers with spoon. Let cool and refrigerate. When completely cold, break up for snacks. For house gift use, use butter instead of oleo. Sprinkle chopped nuts over hot graham crackers.

More junk food

White chocolate bark (liz)

1 ½ lbs almond bark
9 oz snack time pretzels
6 ½ oz can planters redskin Spanish peanuts

Melt almond bark, mix in pretzels and peanuts. Spoon on wax paper and cool in refrigerator. Store in refrigerator or freezer. Use as desired.

Sangria

In a pitcher combine ¼ cup of sugar
1 cup water
1 orange thinly sliced
1 lime thinly sliced
1 lemon thinly sliced
1 bottle red or white wine
6 oz soda water and 18 ice cubes

Dissolve sugar in water in a large pitcher or bowl. Add fruit and wine, plus the ice cubes. Stir until cold. Add sparkling water. Serve putting some of the fruit in each cup or goblet.

Variation: combine the juice of 2 limes, 2 lemons, and 2 oranges with 1/3 cup sugar syrup. Then add one bottle dry red wine and the ice cubes and soda water to taste. Serve the sangria in tall glasses with lime, lemon, and orange slices.

Favorite beef jerky

1 ½ lbs beef   ¼ c soy sauce
1 T Worcestershire sauce   ¼ t pepper

¼ t garlic powder   ½ t onion powder
1/8 t grated nutmeg   ¼ t ground ginger

Chuck, brisket or flank steak can be used. Remove all gristle and fat from meat. Cut meat across the grain 1/8 -1/4 inch thick. For easier cutting, freeze meat and thaw enough to slice easily.

Mix together remaining ingredients and pour over meat. Refrigerate covered for five hrs or overnight. Arrange meat in a single layer on dehydrator trays or a SLOW oven. Dry about five hrs or overnight. Yield about six ounces.

Granola

5 cups oatmeal   1 cup chopped almonds
1 cup sesame seed   1 cup sunflower seeds
1 cup coconut   1 cup instant powder milk
1 cup wheat germ   1 cup honey
1 cup corn oil   2 cups cut mixed dried fruit

Blend all dry ingredients except fruit. Warm honey and oil and add to cereal mix. Combine well. Spread on cookie sheets and bake at 250. Stir occasionally until brown. Add fruit after baking is completed. To dry the granola, mix all the ingredients and spread on trays in SLOW oven. Dry mixture overnight. Store the granola when cool in a tight container. Makes about 12 cups.

Clamburgers

One 10 oz can minced clams, ½ cup cracker meal. 1 t mustard, a little pepper, one egg, 1 thinly sliced green onion; Drain liquid from clams add meal, egg, mustard and pepper. Drop from spoon into hot fat (lard or bacon drippings) spread mixture with back of spoon. Five minutes on each side. You'll get 4-5 nice little burgers. *Just a snack when you're going about some serious cooking.*

Frozen strawberry dessert

8 oz philadelphia cream cheese, 10 oz strawberries unsweetened, one cup xxx sugar, ½ c pecans. Mix together, spread in 8 x 10 inches glass pan and freeze. Serve in 2 x 2 inch squares.

Chef's salad

6 c torn salad greens (romaine, Boston, Bibb, iceberg lettuce) ½ red onion, chopped, ½ cup each slivered boiled ham and Swiss cheese, radish slices and pitted black olives. One cup each halved cherry tomatoes and sliced cauliflorets; 3 hard-cooked eggs, halved.

Arrange greens in large bowl and sprinkle with red onion. Arrange ham and cheese slivers, radish slices, olives, cherry tomatoes, cauliflorets and egg halves in rows on greens. At the table toss with dressing and serve at once. Makes 6 servings.

Vinaigrette dressing; combine ½ cup oil, ¼ cup wine vinegar, ½ t salt and freshly ground pepper to taste.

You may substitute slivers of tongue, turkey or chicken, sliced cukes, tomato wedges, red onion rings, artichoke hearts, sardines or anchovies for some of the ingredients in above recipe.

Stewed celery

One bunch of celery, after having picked out white for the table, cut all but the leaves in small pieces. Boil until tender with a little salt; drain well. Make sauce of one cup milk with 1 T butter and 2 T flour. Turn celery into the sauce and stir well. Season to taste and serve hot.

Fried apples

Wash apples. Cut in ½ inches slices without peeling. Dip in sugar then in flour and fry brown in hot buter.

Sweet and sour tomato aspic

4 cups tomato juice
3 or 4 chunks green pepper
2 dashes soy sauce salt and pepper
2 boxes (3oz each) lemon gelatin
1 cup finely diced celery
1 cup sliced pitted black olives
1 large avocado, peeled and sliced
salad greens
½ cup each mayonnaise and dairy sour cream
paprika

Bring tomato juice to boil with green pepper and soy sauce. Remove pepper and season juice with salt and pepper to taste. Pour over gelatin and stir until dissolved. Add celery, olives and avocado and pour into two quart ring mold or other large mold. Chill until firm and unmold on greens. Serve with mayonnaise and sour cream mixed together and sprinkle with paprika. Serves six.

Variation: cut recipe in half then fill several soup cans with aspic. Chill; unmold, slice into 1/1 ½ inch rounds and serve on salad greens with dollop of above cream dressing.

Basic ham loaf

1 lb ground ham (2 cups)
1 lb. fresh ground pork (2 cups)
1 cup dry bread crumbs (*watch it if you use cracker crumbs, they often result in too salty a dish*)
2 eggs
1 cup milk

Combine all ingredients thoroughly. Pack lightly into 9x5x6 inch loaf pan. Bake in preheated oven for one hour at 350.

Russian cream

1pint sweet cream (half & half or whipping cream may be used)
1- ½ cups granulated sugar
1 T (1 envelope) unflavored gelatin
1 cup cold water
2 t vanilla
1 pint sour cream

Soften gelatin in water. Place sweet cream and sugar in top of double boiler. Heat until sugar is dissolved. Add water and gelatin mixture. Allow to cool. When cold and beginning to thicken, fold in vanilla and sour cream which has been beaten until smooth. Pour into sherbet glasses. Place in refrigerator. When firm top with tablespoon of red raspberries. Either frozen or fresh berries may be used. The latter should be sweetened to taste.

Split pea soup

In a kettle, sauté ½ lb. lean salt pork, diced, over moderate heat until about 2 T of the fat is rendered, add 2 onions, minced, one cup minced celery and sauté the mixture until the onions are softened. Add 8 cups cold water, 2 cups dried split peas, 1t thyme, and 1 bay leaf; bring the liquid to a boil over moderate heat, and simmer mixture covered for 1 ½ hrs or until peas are very tender. Simmer the soup uncovered for about 20 mins more. Remove bay leaf and stir in 2 T minced parsley.

BREAKFAST MENUS

Breakfast recipes

1. Toad in Hole, orange juice, coffee or milk

    Fry one pound of sausage links. Start them in a skillet with a cup of water, prick sausages and turn them as they are cooking. As the water evaporates, sausages will brown. Set them a side and keep them warm.

    Make Yorkshire pudding: 1 cup milk,   2 eggs

                                     1 cup flour   ½ t salt

    Mix salt and flour and add milk gradually to form smooth paste; then add eggs and beat two minutes with egg beater, or electric mixer. Cover bottom of pyrex dish with about four T butter (hot). Pour batter into hot pan and arrange cooked sausages on top of batter and bake for 20 minutes at 450. If pudding is baked in a pyrex pan then temperature must be 425. Cut into serving pieces and serve with syrup.

2. Creamed Chipped beef on Toast, sliced oranges, milk or coffee

    8 oz. chipped beef – pull apart and soak in cold water five minutes. Melt 3 T butter, add 3 T flour and stirring constantly add two cups milk. Add the beef and simmer all until mixture thickens. Serve beef on hot buttered toast. I used to add two sliced hard boiled eggs to stretch this and for additional nourishment.

    Peel and slice California oranges. Serve separately in fruit dishes.

3. Sausage nests with eggs, fried apples, buttered toast, milk or coffee

    1 to 1 ½ pounds of Ekrich smoked sausage or another favorite brand which has been smoked in natural casing. Peel sausage and crumble it. Do this with your hands. Frizzle it lightly in a skillet. Now make a nest of sausage meat in each muffin tin; make a depression in which you drop a raw egg. Add a little salt and pepper to egg and a thin slice of butter topping each egg. Bake in 300-325 oven 10-15 minutes or until eggs are done. Lift nests out with slotted spoon and allow one or more per person as needed.

4. Lamb kidneys with scrambled eggs, toast, grapefruit, milk or coffee

    These are hard to get in any usable amount. Four will do for two or three adults. This is not a favorite of young children, but you will have the scrambled eggs and toast with strawberry or raspberry jam. Split kidneys in half the long way. Pare and trim them, cook them in cold water for five minutes. Cut each half in 4 pieces. Fry quickly in butter with a sprinkling of caraway seeds. Stir with a wooden spoon until juices have evaporated. Kidneys are then done. Kidneys must be cooked a short time or for several hours; they are tender after a few minutes' cooking but soon toughen and then need hours of cooking to again make them tender. Salt. Serve in warm dish. Fry scrambled eggs in a separate dish. Add ½ cup light cream to 6 eggs, mix lightly and pour into hot buttered pan and stir until whites are set. Season with salt and pepper and sprinkle with chopped chives. The amount of eggs you scramble depends on size of family; allow one per child and two for each adult. Serve at once.

5. Scrambled eggs with Swiss cheese, toast, cantaloupe, milk and/or coffee. Scramble

required number of eggs, and a bit of light cream, and cut thin slice of Swiss cheese into strips and add to eggs. Allow about 2T for each two eggs. Fry slowly in buttered skillet until whites are set and cheese is softening. Now turn and fry other side, like a large pancake. I do not mix the eggs and cheese while they're cooking so cheese doesn't burn. Eggs will be soft and creamy. Allow a quarter of cantaloupe per person. If you grow your own, give them a half.

6. Cut up Ham with scrambled eggs, orange juice, English muffins, milk/coffee. Cut up sandwich ham slices in small pieces, and heat them in butter in skillet. Do not brown them. Pour scrambled eggs over ham pieces, mix gently and cook until whites are set. Easy on the salt. Toasted and buttered English muffins are delicious with this.

7. Soft boiled egg, toast, grapefruit
Do you have a friend who does not mix meat and dairy dishes? This is a perfect breakfast. Allow 2-3 eggs per person. Large eggs fresh out of the refrigerator take six minutes to boil so whites are cooked and yolks are runny. If you have them room temperature, five minutes is ok. Put pat of butter in each warm bowl, and drop eggs on top. Salt and pepper-*we like the rough ground kind.* Serve buttered toast with homemade jam. After you have prepared the grape fruit, sprinkle with sugar, unless it's a Texas pink one.

8. French pancakes, sliced oranges and grapefruit, bacon, milk/coffee.

One cup flour	½ t salt
5T powdered sugar	1 cup milk
2 eggs	

Mix dry ingredients, add milk, stir until perfectly smooth. Add eggs, beat thoroughly and cook in hot buttered pan. Cook on one side. When edges are cooked and mixture begins to puff, turn and cook other side. Spread with thin layer of homemade apple sauce or syrup. Buy bacon which is nicely marbled and the meat is pink. Fry slowly, turning frequently but do not allow it to cook until meat is hard or bacon is brown. Peel fruit, remove tough membranes, cut up sections and add sugar to taste.

9. Apple pancake, sausages or sausage pancakes, cranberry juice, milk/coffee

1 ½ cups flour	1 ½ t baking soda
2 cups sugar	1 peeled apple
1 large egg	2 cups buttermilk

Mix dry ingredients, add buttermilk and egg. Now shave one medium apple into batter. Fry in greased pan (bacon drippings). Serve with fried sausage patties and syrup. The sliced apple in the batter is an interesting, flavorful addition.

10. Breakfast biscuits baked in brown sugar and butter. Bake in hot oven fro10 min. invert on chop plate and cover with the pan or deep lid to keep hot and prevent drying

out. Serve piping hot with bacon strips, o.j. and milk/coffee. Pass the butter.

11. Chicken livers with bacon, buttered toast, sliced orange, coffee and or milk.
Clean livers and cut each live (2 halves) in half. Wrap half a thin slice of bacon around each piece and fasten with a toothpick. Put in a broiler, place over a dripping pan and bake in hot oven until bacon is crisp, turning once during cooking.

12. Waffles, maple syrup, orange juice, coffee

1 – ½ cups flour	1 cup milk
3 T baking powder	2 egg yolks
½ t salt	2 egg whites
2 t sugar	3 to 4 T melted butter

Mix and sift dry ingredients. Add milk gradually, egg yolks well beaten, and fold in egg whites beaten stiff. Cook on electric waffle iron. Serve with maple syrup. It's still available but more costly.

13. French toast, breakfast sausage links, grapefruit, milk/coffee
For every four slices of regular white bread, make batter of two eggs and ½ cup milk. Beat batter well while an ample portion of butter is frying in the pan. Get the butter good and hot (but don't burn) before putting each piece of batter-soaked bread in the pan. Sprinkle the toast, hot from the pan, with powdered sugar. It forms a candy-like glaze.

14. Breakfast Quiche, strawberries, coffee.
Plain pastry for one 9" pie shell
1 c shredded cheddar or Swiss cheese
2 c light cream or evaporate milk
8 slices bacon, cooked and diced
6 eggs, beaten
1 t onion salt

Line pie pan with pasty, set aside. Brown bacon slices, drain and dice. Cool. Combine eggs, cheese and onion salt. Stir in diced bacon, and cream and blend well. Pour egg mixture into pie shell and bake in preheated 375 oven for 30-35 minutes until center tests done. Serve hot in wedges.

16. Eggs Benedict
8 slices smoked ham (Can.)
4 eggs
2 English muffins split, toasted and buttered
4 custard cups (6 oz.) size

Arrange 2 slices ham, break and slip egg into the cup. Bake until eggs all done. Loosen from side of cups and slide onto muffin ½ Hollandaise sauce optional.

SOUPS

Lentil soup

1 meaty ham hock which has been washed
1 stalk celery
1 carrot
1 small onion
1 ½ cups lentils
6 cups water
1 med. potato

Cook ham hock in water until done. Take it out and set it aside. Pick over lentils; then wash them. Put them into the broth along with thinly sliced celery, carrot and onion and simmer for about 1-1/2 hrs. now add potatoes cut into small cubes and continue cooking for another half hour.

Cut meat and skin off ham hock into small pieces and drop into soup. Serve soup with buttered rye bread. Serves 4

Chicken soup

One large chicken (4 lbs)
One large white onion
Half carrot, stalk of celery with leaves, two sprigs parsley, half parsnip all tied together.
Two-three quarts of cold water

Wash chicken, and pull out chicken fat. Use this later for cream sauce. Place chicken and vegetables into pot and cover with about 3 quarts water. Cook slowly for an hour and a half (add salt last half hour). Strain the broth. (Remove vegetables and mix them with your dog's food). Serve chicken whole on platter to the family or skin and bone it and use it for chicken a la king, or chicken salad or sandwiches etc.

This is what my son in law calls Jewish penicillin.

Now here are ways to vary the chicken soup:

1.   Ladle four or six cups of soup into a pan, bring to a boil and add a handful of fine noodles. Cook 5 min. add chopped parsley.
2.   Ladle four or six cups of soup into a pan, add handful of diagonal thin slices of

wax beans and about five thinly sliced mushrooms. Simmer for ten minutes and serve.

3.   Ladle four or six cups of soup into a pan, add one cup cooked barley and pepper and heat.

4.   Ladle four or six cups of soup into a pan, add one cup cooked rice, heat ; add chick peas and thinly cut chicken.

5.   Ladle four or six cups of soup into a pan, add handful of fine noodles plus handful of fresh peas. Cook for about 5-8 mi. and serve.

6.   Ladle four or six cups of soup into a pan, add little liver dumplings, cook for about 10-12 minutes and serve.

Liver dumplings: one large slice beef liver scraped with knife. Discard gristle. Mash one clove garlic with ½ t salt, add one egg and half cup bread crumbs and mix thoroughly. Now add grated liver and pepper to it. Make small dumplings. Roll them in crumbs if too moist. Drop them into boiling broth and simmer for 10-12 minutes. Serve 3 or 4 in a bowl. *This is very tasty and a great favorite with the opposite sex.*

7.   Ladle four or six cups of soup into a pan, add egg drops to boiling broth. Egg drops: ½ cup flour, ½ t salt, one egg. Mix thoroughly. Dough should be runny. Allow to rest for 20 mins. Drop from teaspoon, dipped in cold water, into boiling broth. If dough sticks to bottom of pan, loosen with wooden spoon. All is done when egg drops come to top. Add chopped parsley.

Oxtail soup with Tripe

1 oxtail	one large cubed potato
1 neck beef	
8 cups water	½ cup barley
½ cup each carrot, onion, celery	1 lb. tripe
½ t salt – few grains cayenne	

Cut oxtail between joints, wash, drain, sprinkle with salt and pepper, dredge with flour and try in butter ten minutes to brown. Add water and beef and barley, simmer 2 hours. Then add vegetables and taste if necessary, add water simmer until vegies are soft, add salt and cayenne.

Cook tripe separately. Cut into strips 1" x 1/3" and add at end. Rub marjoram between palms over each serving.

Asparagus Soup

3 cups white stock (chicken or veal)
1 can asparagus or half lb. fresh asparagus cut in small pieces and cooked
in stock; reserve tips and cook these separately
Boil about thirty minutes, and bind with butter and flour cooked together (1/4 c butter
– ¼ c flour)
Add salt, pepper and 2 cups scalded milk, add the tips before serving.

Beefsteak Pie

Cut remnants of cold broiled steak or roast beef in one inch cubes. Cover with boiling
water, add one-half onion and cook slowly one hour. Remove onion, thicken gravy with
flour diluted with cold water, and season with Lowry's salt and pepper. Add potatoes cut
in one-fourth inch slices which have been parboiled eight minutes in boiling salted water.
Put in a buttered dish cool, cover with baking powder biscuits or pie crust. Bake in a hot
oven. If covered with pie crust, make several incisions in crust for escape of steam.

Beef Soup

1 large beef shank cut ffrom foreleg, small pieces of beef liver
1 large onion
2 small cloves garlic
12 pepper and allspice corns
2 stalks celery
1 N0. 2 can tomatoes
8 bowls water, salt and pepper

Heat water to boiling; add other ingredients; simmer over low heat for two hours or until
meat is tender. Add salt. Strain and serve with fine noodles. Meat may be served with
horseradish or ketchup. Give the liver to the cat.

Thick Beef Soup

One pound ground chuck
One knuckle bone with trimmings
One thinly sliced onion
Two thinly sliced celery stalks
3 or four cabbage leaves, sliced
two thinly sliced carrots
1 large can tomato juice
2 large cans water
½ cup barley, rinsed

One large cubed potato
1 box frozen mixed vegetables
salt and a bit of pepper

Fill soup pot with water and tomato juice. With your hands mix the ground chuck into the tomato juice and water. Now add all the ingredients except the barley, potato and frozen vegetables. Simmer the soup for two hours; taste for seasoning. Then add barley and cubed potato. Continue cooking for another hour. At the last add the mixed vegetables and cook only another fifteen minutes. The soup should be thick and hearty. If you have a bone gnawer in the family, give him/her the knuckle bone with all that remainder, (and he will never stray).

This soup is particularly good for children. It's nutritious and easy to eat as well as digest; it is attractive. The vegetables still retain their color and the soup looks very appetizing.

This will make enough soup for a family of six for several lunches. Allow it to cool before storing. Be sure not to cover pot completely. Allow steam to escape as it cools, else it will spoil. Store in covered jars in refrigerator. This will make approximately 3 quarts soup.

Milk Soup

(This was a favorite of my Mother's)

Allow a quart of milk to come to the boiling point. (Watch it!) When it begins to bubble, add home made noodles, salt and a small piece of butter. Boil until noodles are done and serve.

Bean Soup (Cathy)

2 cups navy beans soaked overnight or for four hours. Pour off water, add 8 cups water, 1 chopped carrot, one stalk chopped celery, and one meaty ham hock. Bring to boil and simmer until beans are almost done; then add one finely cut potato (One of the mealy ones like an Idaho). Continue cooking this until potatoes are mushy. Taste for seasoning. Cut meat and skin into soup.

Bake the yellow corn bread according to directions on Quaker box. Cut into serving pieces. Place a chunk of corn bread into deep soup bowl, cover with bean soup and add finely sliced helping of Spanish onion on top. The men love this.

Tomato Soup

One quart tomato juice	1 t salt
1 pint water	1 small sliced onion
12 pepper corns	2 T butter
4 cloves	bit of bay leaf

Cook all ingredients except butter for one hour. Strain soup, add butter, serve hot with one tablespoon of salted whipped cream.

Be sure to cook soup in either aluminum or porcelain lined pan. Steel cooking pots destroy the acid in tomatoes, and the whole thing is less than tasty.

Mushroom Chowder

Combine condensed cream of mushroom soup with one can of light cream, one can of sautéed sliced mushrooms, and a few spoonfuls of lightly sautéed onion. Heat and serve. It's good and substantially serves 4.

Tripe Soup

Thoroughly wash tripe, place in a kettle, cover with cold water and boil half an hour. Drain, cover once more with cold water, add salt and allow it to boil until tender. Take it out, cut in thin strips, place them in a kettle, pour good beef soup over them, add minced parsley, butter and flour blended together until brown (a roux). This can be added to the beef and bean soup; delicious

Beef and bean soup

Wash one cup of navy beans (those are the small ones – don't use great northerns.). Place in kettle with a two pound piece of neck beef, sliced onion, carrot and celery. Add two quarts water and let all simmer. When soup ceases foaming add the vegetables and continue cooking 2 ½ to 3 hours. If soup evaporates, add hot water. When done, take out meat, remove from bone, cut up and put back in pot. Finally add handful of noodles. Cook five minutes and serve, with a turn of pepper in each bowl.

Rye Bread Soup

Cut thin slices of rye bread, toast them well, butter them and rub them with cut side of garlic clove. Place bread in pan, pour clear soup (beef) over it, add salt, pepper, and a ¼ t caraway seed. Let all boil together for a few minutes, then add minced parsley and chives. Serve hot.

Chicken Broth

Note: *Some of the chickens do not have the flavor that you remember from your youth. Add a chicken bouillon cube to the broth if it needs help.*

Chicken Velvet: Add half cup sautéed, finely cut mushrooms and one cup of finely cut cooked chicken to 6 cups broth and heat. Now add one cup cream. Season to taste and serve hot.

MEMOIRS

"REMINISCENCES OF A BOHEMIAN- AMERICAN; BORN IN BRNO,
CZECHOSLOVAKIA, 1912; EMIGRATED TO AMERICA, 1922"

Once upon a time a little girl named Augusta Elizabeth Cecelia Chalabala lived in a two room house in Brno, Czechoslovakia with her mama, her aunt Anne, and her uncles,- and her "baba" (little grandmother), who owned the house and the one behind it which she rented out. These are some of her memories of Europe in the early 1900's, and Chicago during the 20's and 30's.

Please note that these memories are in random order. They give a flavor and a feeling of the times, and they are authentic, not imagined or made up.

Siblings of JJ Chalabala

Grandpa (John Joseph) Chalabala

Carl Chalabala died in a concentration camp because he was proud of being a German. He said "I'm not a cheska-bleska" That means" I'm not a Czech flea." When asked to declare his allegiance at the end of World War Two.

Half brothers are:

Fred Konrad (Ferdinand) father of Bertha and Helen.

Leo Konrad

(Bobby threw Leo out of the house when Leo wanted her to polish his army boots! So he must have been on horseback in the calvary.)

The Konrads are from the first father- who died in an accident at work- John Joseph and Carl are from Ignace Chalabala, the 2nd father.

Ivo and Nora Reznichec were educated by the commies- she's a doctor (Carl's granddaughter, Bobby's brother). They have two adopted Russian boys.

Bobby's siblings:

Grandpa got them jobs as:

1. Carl-butcher's apprentice. Grandpa threatened the butcher with bodily harm if he abused Carl who was small and thin.
2. Matt- too proud to be helped. Became a roofer on his own.

3. Alfred – liquer factory. Mixed liquers. He'd lost a lung in WW1, so he couldn't do any heavy work.

4. Anna- day work- worked for a rich family as (Bobby was a weaver by trade) a servant. When her ½ day or whole day off and she came home, she was starving and asked her sister for anything, anything! Bobby responded "Jayzhee smudeeah ("Jesus, Mary and Joseph!") all I have is potatoes!" Bobby told grandpa that Anna was working from dawn to dark and not being fed. She wanted to quit, but they wouldn't let her take her coat!! Grandpa went with her, demanded her coat and took her home.

Later when Bobby was in Chicago, a butcher asked her whether there were any more at home like her. She answered yes, a sister. After meeting grandpa and proving himself worthy, a deal was struck: he would pay for her passage to America and marry her. Anne left home for Hamburg to pick up the boat to come to America. But her boyfriend followed her and they married. Grandpa Chalabala was furious with Anne because he had sent her a visa as well as money to come to America. (Anne's boyfriend had been wounded in the First World War and had lost an eye. And earlier, when he had asked Grandpa's permission to marry Anne, he had been refused because "what would become of Anne if he lost his other eye?") There was no welfare or anything else.

Later she was courted by a young man who had lost an eye in WW1, and when he asked grandpa for her hand in marriage, grandpa said "no, what will happen to her if your other eye is damaged?"

When Bobby was in Europe, a door to door Jewish peddler sold her a pair of scissors that she paid one cent a week for. He asked her father for her hand in marriage. He told her father that "she would never have to work". Her dad said "No!" He married a Jewess and opened a store. His wife sat at the cash register all day long. She even had a wet nurse for her babies.

1922, one of the boys who lived next door to mom in Brno referred to her as "my old lady." Mom had mixed emotions- she was pleased to be noticed, but thought to herself "old lady? I'm only ten!" that was the year she came to America.

Mom was sort of "promised" to the son of the owner of the factory where grandpa was the superintendent. The boy had an" Irish Mail." Mom was fascinated! But he didn't offer to let her try. So she had to just sit there and be silent.

Grandma Chalabala (my Mom's grandma) raised a pig every year and after it was butchered, lived on it for a year. Grandpa John Joe and his brother Carl, decided to help their mom by killing the pig for her. She came home to find them riding its' back stabbing it with a kitchen knife.

Bobby liked to buy a slab of bacon with the skin on at Hillman's in Chicago and roast it. Yum. With sauerkraut and dumplings.

You need one egg for dumplings; noodles; egg drops in chicken soup; frying chicken or frying rabbit.

When Mom was a little girl and attended mass in Brno, she saw a beautiful painting of the Blessed Virgin and because she was so beautiful, laid her only holy card on her altar.

Vienna. When Mom took off her shoes because her shoes hurt her feet, the guard at the park wouldn't let them in because of it! My mom, her mom and her dad. Mom was indignant.

1918 "I have to have my hands free in case we're attacked by bandits." Grandpa's response to mom when she asked him why he walked ahead of her and her mom (Bobby), when Bobby was carrying bundles.

A months' leave from the army when grandpa picked up a grenade and threw it back at the enemy's lines where it exploded.

After the war, grandpa wouldn't hire an apprentice unless he could bring a sack of potatoes or other food every month. There was no food to be had! No matter what $ you had! He was so ashamed he decided to emirate to Russia. Russia was 'the promised land' at that time. Going to night school to learn Russian. (he already spoke German, Czech, Austrian, Polish and Yugoslavian) On the way home from nite school he stopped for a stein of beer at a biergarten and met an acquaintance returned from America with pockets full of dollar bills. "that dumkoff! I wouldn't hire him! If he can make that kind of money, I can make more. I'm going to America!" he told Bobby.

Mom lived on Taboravsca Street in Brno.

At St. Nicholas' day (Dec. 6) the devil and St. Nicholas would stop at each house to check into whether the children had been good. You put a plate in the window and if you were good you got an orange, if you were bad, you got a lump of coal.

Grandpa Chalabala (my grandfather John Joseph) and his brother, Carl, were being bathed in a round wash tub, galvanized metal when the devil came calling, dressed in black and rattling his chains. The two little boys were so terrified that they tipped over the tub of water and ran through the glass door of the room, shattering it. Their mom spanked them. (In those days, the interior rooms of a home were enclosed in etched glass, so that you could have privacy, but light.)

Once when Mom and Grandpa and Bobby were picnicing in a park in the mountains, Mom went for a walk and saw a bear! When she ran to tell her parents, they smiled at her in disbelief, and Grandpa said, "What an imagination she has!"

Grandpa C. would get off the el at 12th and Austin Blvd. and walk a mile home. He could take another el for 7 cents, but wouldn't. He wanted to save the money. He died owning two homes. Paid for.

Grandpa Wiggs taught grandpa C. how to drive a car!

Grandpa C. bought a house next to his in Berwyn Illinois. When Grandpa Wiggs died unexpectedly, leaving his widow- Mary Casey – his son, Robert and wife Ruth and daughter Rae Jane and her boyfriend with nothing. All of them! Grandpa C took them in so that they would not "be on Jims' back."

Grandma Smejkal had two brothers who kept horses for the military-horses that were discharged. Each horse was in top condition; each had it's own stableman who slept with the horse. Occasionally the horses' owner would appear in full regalia to wipe his gloved hands over the beast, checking for dust in its' fur coat. After a year, if the horse was in perfect condition it belonged to the caretaker.

Mom wasn't raised to speak. She could only answer questions so her observations alone are the basis for these notes and memoirs. She says that you could smell the freedom in the air when you came to America.

Grandpa and Grandma Smejkal, Bobby and mom (Grandpa was at WW1, eastern front. Serbia and Turkey)

Matt, Karl, Alfred and Aunt Anna all lived together.

During WW1 mom spent the days with the Smejkals, and the evenings with Grandpa Ignatz and Grandma Josephine Chalabala and her own Mom, of course.

Bobby raised chickens at Grandpa Chalabala's —she'd shoo them out to the train tracks during the day. In the morning, she'd carry her little lunch bucket to work.

Grandpa Smejkal raised rabbits and occasionally butchered one. Each rabbit had a back cut into four pieces, four legs and a liver. So each person had one piece of meat.

After WW1, in a house across the street from grandma Smejkals' in Europe, Bobby invited Mom's kindergarten teacher to lunch and served her cooked spinach and a whole hard boiled egg sliced over it. The teacher was overwhelmed! A whole egg for herself!

When President Hoover sent oleo and corn meal to starving Europe, Bobby was insulted! She wanted lard and flour. (Bobby baked corn bread, and mom liked it)

Mom saw President Woodrow Wilson in 1918 when she was six years old. Her mom gave her a bouquet of roses (that she had grown on her rose trees)"give this to the president" to give to the president. When he drove by in an open touring car in top hat and tails she threw the bouquet at him (heaved the bouquet at him) it hit him. He smiled, was very pleased and tipped his hat at her! Mom wore a dress covered by a little green and pink roses print pinafore. Mom called this little pinafore her "sauerkraut apron." Bobby's dad liked mom (grandpa Smejkal) and he would occasionally give her a small coin to spend at the horse butchers across the street from her home. Grandpa Smejkal named the little apron she wore that day.

Bobby would not buy horse meat; it was "low class".

Grandpa Smejkal was a farmer who could neither read nor write, married to a school superintendents' daughter who could. She moved him to the city and he became a blacksmith. He was a red head and very handsome.

Smejkal means "to tip your hat". Smetana means "creame."

Grandpa Smejkal owned his own home in Brno CZ. which had a separate 2 room cottage on the back of the property. He rented it.

When grandpa wrote to uncle Fred (Konrad) asking for a visa, aunt Josephine, uncle Fred's wife talked him "into sending it" so uncle Fred had to become grandpa's sponser.

To pay for passage, Bobby sold everything: the furniture, the dishes, linens, silverware. (Bobby and grandpa rented a house across the street from Grandpa Smejkal. He had only been home from the war a couple of years)

Grandpa bought his ticket and went to Hamburg Germany, where he discovered he needed 40 kronin- the price had changed. He had no way to raise 40 kronin. As he's walking along the dock worrying, he sees seamen playing a game and joins in. He wins 40 kronin, grabs it and runs for his life! Aboard the ship he finds the toilet facilities revolting. So he wouldn't go at all. He wouldn't sleep with the passengers because they were dirty and crowded. So he tied himself to the mast and slept on the deck. When the ship arrived in New York harbor, it was sent to Boston harbor because there were too many ships in New York. Grandpa spent his first night in America in jail because there was no place else to put the emigrants.

In the trenches, the opposing army threw a hand grenade into his trench, grandpa picked it up and threw it back! He got a week off to come home.

Second in the army of Austria for bayoneting. He got another week off to come home. And a medal which mom has.

Grandpa didn't want to stay in America. He wanted to return to Europe but Bobby said she would divorce him if he returned. Big excitement! She wanted to come to America with mom. So grandpa relented and sent 2 visas. He paid a man he knew to come with Bobby and mom to protect them on the boat. When the man came to see grandpa on Harvey street Mom told grandpa that the guy never did anything, grandpa said "I know but here you are."

As soon as Bobby could, she enrolled herself and grandpa in night classes to become American citizens. A year later when he was to renounce his Czech citizenship he hesitated and said "it's the fatherland" Bobby said "fatherland! What did the fatherland ever give you but a war and a starving child! Sign that paper!" that's how they became Americans.

In the usa, grandpa bought a $400 piano and mom was to learn to play. Bobby hired a teacher for $1/lesson, who rode the el and walked to mom's house to give her a piano lesson. Bobby always gave the woman a cup of coffee and a piece of Kolačky before she left.

Mom entered a piano competition advertised in the Chicago tribune. She played "poet and peasant." Grandpa came to watch her- it was in the Chicago Theater. (Mom always entered the contests in the Chicago tribune- Raymond, a kid in her class always criticized her efforts. But she enjoyed all the excitement.)

Mom didn't win, but Mom met the Jewish woman at Tell-a Type who had won the piano competition where the prize was a new home and playing for the silent films. The winner never got to play in the theater because "talkies" came in.

Grandpa told mom during the Depression, that she was to be careful because people all up and down the street were losing their homes, and grandpa and Bobby and mom all had jobs.

After the WW1, no food. Grandpa is walking to the frontier to buy black market potatoes. He takes mom with him and coming home puts her on top of the sack of potatoes which he slung over his back and he tells her to be quiet. So she went to sleep. He told Bobby that she was his protection – an armed guard on the border would not pay too much attention to a man walking with a little child.

Mom bought Bobby a bag of gladiola bulbs for 35 cents in the company store. Bobby was so pleased! She gave mom a bouquet to take to work. Dr. Fruth, "president of flower club" saw mom's bouquet on her desk and came to see what Bobby was doing. The gladiolas were so huge. Bobby had a deal with the milkman, who bought her horse manure which she spread on her garden in the fall. It lay under the snow all winter, and in the spring she turned it under.

In Berwyn Illinois (Chicago)

Mom named her grade school, the "Abraham Lincoln" school and mom picked out the school colors: grey and blue. Lerner's dress shop in the loop. All dresses priced $7.99 or less. The dress that she loved was blue and grey and so she suggested these colors.

When Grandpa came to America he sent mom a violin and then an illustrated fairytale book which she loved. She must have told her teacher about the book because the teacher asked her if she would like to share a story with the class. Mom told the story to the class with gestures! She drew the sword and saved the princess! The class loved it!

She couldn't bring it with her to America because she couldn't ask for it. In Europe at that time, children were not allowed to speak unless spoken to and then, they were only allowed to answer the question. Period. No conversation, ever. If they opened their mouths, they were slapped, hard.

Mr. Winters was a teacher of mom's at Morton High. She had a photographic memory and could repeat verbatim the text. He was glad to have her as a "student" as apposed to a "pupil." He was going down the rows of the class asking questions of each until he reached mom. "There's no use asking Ms. Chalabala, she won't know." "Oh, I do Mr. Winters, I do." At which point she answered verbatim. He asked her if she was reading from the text. She had left her book in another classroom.

Grandpa Smejkad and the rabbits. Grandpa raised rabbits and we'd have one once a month, cut into seven pieces, one piece for each person. It was after the WW1, and thee wasn't enough to eat. Grandpa Smejkad put winter pears up in the attic on 6 inches of straw to ripen. It took a couple of months.

After the war, grandpa returned minus his ring finger, one out of forty who survived. He was on the eastern front. I remember him telling me that Serbia was the end of bread and beginning of stone. There were snakes everywhere. He and his men marched all through the day and nite to escape the Turks. They marched so long that they could only think of two things: the next step and what the Turks would do to them if they were caught. They ran out of food and came upon an onion field and ate them all. They escaped the turks.

Grandpa sent Bobby a box made of wooden matches, lined in dark blue velvet and on the top a post card of Bosnia Hertzegovina- where the war started when Archduke Ferdinand was assassinated on grandpa's day off- he was part of the private guard for Archduke Ferdinand, and if he hadn't had a day off, he would have been killed too.

When mom was dismissed from AT&T duing the depression after two weeks she got a job at Tell a Type. Mom walked a mile and took an el to the loop, another el north and then walked a mile after getting off. Four miles of walking each day!

Private Secretary to Mr. Straw? No, mom didn't want to be in a private office with him-even though it was more money and closer to home.

Mr. Whitfield who was boss at "Tell a Type" asked her(at her going away to get married party) "if she was aware of the importance of her undertaking?" to which she replied, " I certainly am; I am a Catholic."

Grandpa Ignace Chalabala (Grandpa's Dad) married Josephine Konrad (a widow with children) when he and his girlfriend broke up. His girlfriend married another man. Many years later when he was 80 and a widower, they remet and married!

Antonie Smejkal (weaver, cooking school)

Ann Smejkal (maid, factory)

Carl Smejkal (butcher) Reznichek Nora is his daughter

Alfred Smejkal (liquer mixer)

Matthew Smejkal (roofer, made tunk)

Stanislov Smejkal (bartender in Pilsen- gave Mom gold jewelry)

Mom had to make beer every Friday. Mom had to be home on Thursdays at 3pm to make noodles

Every week Grandpa deposited his pay check in the bank and paid all the bills. When he decided to move to Indianapolis and went to the bank to close his account, George Vishstein, the bank owner, asked grandpa what he was going to do with 1401 Gunderson. Grandpa said, "I don't know." Mr. Vishstein said, 'Rent it to me.' 135/month for 19 years until Mr. Vishstein died.

Whenever Bobby needed money for something like curtains, she'd get a job. Bobby worked in a little lunchroom in the "Boston store". A girl in a tellers' cage took your money and gave you a pink, green, blue or yellow slip- one for coffee, one for pie, one for ice-cream or a combination. You gave your ticket to the ladies behind the counter, who gave you the item. Only the woman in the tellers' cage touched the money.

Circa 1930:

"Gooey Sam's" – oriental(Carl Berquist's parents took them)

"Mann's Rainbow" –broiled lobster; frog's legs'; crab cakes in an abalone shell

"Palmer House" –formal dinner

"Kranz Viennese" coffee and cake for the rich ladies, after leaving the theatre. Then they went home to their maids.

When mom was going to the art institute once a week she went to "The Triangle Café" for supper. She got a slice of ham, sweet potatoes and coleslaw for 35 cents. 25 cents carfare for 3 rides: to work, to loop for dinner and out and home.

Classes cost $2/week. Bobby got $8/week from mom.

At the art institute mom drew in charcoal "Views of the bust of Caesar"-"if you can draw this, you can draw anything." "When I got up in the morning and looked out the window, I felt the world had been created for me." Steamboat Springs. Her instructor's words.

Mom was working during the depression until she was finally let go. She got her last paycheck and took it home to grandpa (Berwyn, Illinois) and gave it all to him. He used it to pay taxes on their home- it saved their home.

There's a big difference between 13 and 14. when you are 13 you play with dolls and jump into flooded basements for a summer swim, clean out chicken coops to use as a girls' club. But when you're 14, you go to high school and put away your skates and dolls and loose your girlhood friends over a boy. In this case mom and her best friend Lillian Liska, Joe Serpico, a cute well groomed upperclassman. His father was a tailor, who made his clothes for him. But a tailor wasn't as good as grandpa. Who was a master machinist and ran a factory, so mom dropped Joe Serpico, and of course lost Lillian Liska forever.

Grandma Smejkal was the daughter of a school teacher and she knew how to read and write!

Grandpa and Grandma Smejkal owned a house on Tabor street in Brno. The house was on the street and behind it there was a separate house which was rented out. There was an outside toilet for all. Beyond the rental house was the second yard with a garden for veggies and flowers.

The first yard which was between the main house and the rental house held the rabbit hutch, the outside toilet, the pig house (sty), the rain barrel (which caught the laundry water, drinking water, cooking water, bathing water.) There was no indoor plumbing.

Grandpa Smejkal was a farmer, but sold his farm and moved to the city at his wife's request. He became a blacksmith. He had red hair and a red moustache and occasionally would slip mom a kronin (10 cents) to go across the street to the horse butcher, where she bought a piece of horse sausage- delicious! Bobby refused to go to the horse butcher because it was too low class.

Grandpa and grandma Chalabala lived near the train. The house had indoor plumbing (!) a kitchen, a parlor, an extra bedroom for Carl (who died in a concentration camp during the WW2) and an outside well which grandpa Ignace let the neighbors use. Grandpa Ignace was a bookkeeper and when he became aged he as let go. Mom's dad was furious over his dad's mistreatment. Grandpa said, "when a man works all his life for you, you do not put him out; you find something for him to do-give him a broom to push, let him sweep the sidewalk." The owner of the company that let his father go wrote to grandpa years later asking for a visa- to escape Hitler- and grandpa refused. Mom said, "but that was years ago…" Grandpa responded "keep out of this."

Apparently, mom sang all the time, "they missed the little bird who sang in the garden." Grandma Smejkal had a neighbor who had a Queen Ann cherry tree which hung over the fence and every year the neighbors gave a basket of cherries to Bobbi for mom-"the little bird"

The first thing grandpa sent from the USA to Bobby for mom was money to buy her a violin! She took group lessons, but since grandma Smejkal couldn't stand the sounds of practice, mom couldn't practice at home so she made no progress and eventually the lessons were stopped.

They came home soaking wet- by the time they reached their home, they were dry. That's how hot it was that summer in Chicago. Lillian's Mom said, "tsk, tsk, tsk you dirty kids. Why don't you go clean out the chicken coop?" so they did! But the ceiling was only about four feet tall, so they abandoned the idea of a girls' club since they couldn't stand up once it was cleaned.

Grandpa bought a little billy goat as a pet for mom. He would let the little ram butt him. They already had a dog, buffy, and a pussy cat, Mitzi, which everyone enjoyed. Eventually the little goat ended up as diner because he was simply not a pet.

1. Photos needed: photo of mom and three children; photo of Grandpa's clock-sears and company; 1920 photo of the glass lamp from their first Xmas; photo of Matt's trunk that came to America in 1922; photos of mom and Bobbu on their passport

Lillian Krenek, Rudy's sister, was all dressed up for a date. She had a black buster brown haircut, black eyelashes, blue eyes and an orange tangerine velvet dress. She told mom and mom's friend, Lil, that she had to remember that it was impolite to clean your plate. She would have to leave a piece of sandwich on her dish.

Grandma Smejkal's two brothers bid for horses retired from the cavalry- in Czechoslovakia- a couple of times over a year the army officer came to rub white gloves over the horse to check its' condition. Each horse had its' own groom who cleaned it, fed it and slept in the same stall. So the brothers paid for the horse and its' upkeep for one year... after which the horse was theirs.

Frank came over to see grandpa to get his brother, Carl, a job. When mom (age 18) opened the door, Frank was smitten. Later, Grandpa asked Mom's opinion of Carl. Mom told Grandpa that Carl was okay - that he should give Carl a job.

Grandpa and mom went to see "King Kong" together. They had a wonderful time!

Carl B took mom to see "Frankenstein". In the part of the movie when Frankenstein was approaching a little girl, mom was so upset she threw up – once in the theater and once on the way out.

Hugo Beranek took mom to an afternoon performance- a matinee- of the ballet Russe. After the performance Hugo took mom backstage to meet Saul Hurock – who made a pass at her.

Hugo's friend, MacAdam, who was terribly handsome, left the gang when "the Normandy" docked in Chicago. He said" I'll see you guys" and left to join the crew. with the idea of marrying a wealthy woman. He never returned.

1401 Gunderson, Berwyn, Illinois, Bobby's dream house.

Carl introduced Mom to Chinese food, "Gooey Sam's. Afterwards they went to a Chinese mart that sold clothing and jewelry. No one in sight. Carl said "pick out something, when Mom picked out a jade heart on a gold chain, people came out from behind silk kimonos hanging on the walls. $298.00! not $2.98!

"Kranz" a Viennese coffee and cake shop in the Chicago loop. Handmade candies. Bowed windows 8'x3' each of curved glass in which stood crystallized sugar life sized statues- mom remembers a life sized sugar nymph in the window.

After an afternoon matinee the wealthy ladies would come for coffee and cake.

Mom went to "Kranz" a couple of times with Carl Berquist who had graduated from Chicago university. His family had a full time maid. His dad was an important man at Bell Labs. His dad came to check out mom and the family, Carl's family loved Mom. They were wealthy, but he was plain. (Joanna hill roses, yellow with pink center corsage. Talisman roses for Carl's sister's corsage.) So Mom married dad who was handsome and she was an artist, of course. And Dad was a graduate of Purdue university, he had a Masters in chemical engineering.

Frank Lutha- Purdue graduate. Father owned a milk dairy. Frank was fat. He worked for Otis elevator in Alaska. He met mom when he came to see Grandpa about getting a job for his brother, Carl.

Rudy Krenek- the son of the man who built and owned the home Grandpa and Bobby and mom rented (Harvey st.) when they first came to America. He was also a builder. But too sweet. Mom was afraid she'd run over him roughshod. Mom would borrow his bike and smash it regularly. He would never get mad. They played "Piggy move up," a pitcher, catcher and players on the intersection's four corners.

Hugo Beranek the captain of the junior college football team who said "life is too short to work" Hugo and his little brother George each had a coupe with a rumble seat and they attended Morton Junior college. Mom was there too because Morton High School was part of MJC.

In Europe, they Dye Easter eggs with onion (yellow) water, tea (yellow/tea) water, beet (magenta) water, spinach (green) water.

Berwyn IL, an outsider wasn't welcome. Down the street from mom lived a white man and a Chinese woman who had an exquisite baby and one chicken which laid an egg a day for the baby. The neighbors "persuaded" the couple to leave after six months.

My mom's parents bought a piano. It was delivered in its own box. Mom and Lillian Liska (means "Fox") her best friend dragged the piano box down the block to a construction site that had flooded from the spring rains. They threw it into the basement of the house and jumped in after it! What fun they had climbing on it and jumping off into the water.

Uncle Matthew hid money in his mother's chest- mom stole it. Grandma Smejkal got it and put it back without telling Bobby.

After the war grandpa introduced women into the factory because so many men had died in the WW1. He had men working on one side of the factory and women on the other side – no hanky panky.

Bobby went to a convent to learn how to cook. Businessmen came in for lunch. One of the doctors showed an interest in her. She said to mom, "but of course I had you." And shook her head to indicate there was no interest on her part.

She bring home a small piece of cake and give it to mom, who'd save it to trade with Carl who'd bring home a tiny end of the sausage for her. Carl was the youngest of Bobbi's brothers, so he was tiny physically due to no food available during the WW1. Grandpa found Carl an apprenticeship with a butcher- three years to learn a trade- he threatened the butcher with a beating if he mistreated Carl.

Grandpa got Alfred a job mixing liquors because h couldn't do anything heavy. He had been in the WW1 and lost a lung.

Bobby raised a pig in the backyard garden. It had its' own little house that was washed daily. It could come up the back stairs to ask for dinner. When it was time to go to the abattoir Grandpa killed it, loaded it on a two wheel cart which he had made and took it to the butcher to be cut up. Later, Grandpa sold the cart to his neighbor.

My dad's grandfather, Robert Wiggs, who married Lizzy Beltz, was one of two Scotch orphans who were brought to America by an unknown person or persons. His brother died.

Robert Wiggs married Lizzy Belts (German-"Pennsylvania Dutch")

John Custer Wiggs married Mary Casey from (County Cork)

James William Wiggs and Robert Wiggs and Rae Jane Wiggs, children of John Custer Wiggs and Mary Casey.

Stayed with one grandma during the afternoons and spent nights at the other grandma's.

Ignace Chalabala's father wanted Ignace to punish grandpa because he farted while playing. The little boy was only three or so. Ignace refused, saying "you can't put an old head on young shoulders." The grandfather said he'd leave and never return if the child went unpunished. The grandfather never returned.

She named her new school in Chicago "Abraham Lincoln" and chose the school colors (worn as ribbons on the children's left shoulders) blue and grey. The teachers thought she had chosen civil war colors and were very impressed. But actually she had seen a blue and grey suit in the window of the "Lerners" store in the loop and that was the reason for her choice.

Aunts Helen and Bertha were Uncle Fred's daughters (Konrads) Aunt Helen married a descendant of Alexander Hamilton named Heald. They wed right out of high school. Stayed married three ears. Had no children. Helen supported him.

Next Helen married Whelan. Had Joan. Whelan died, leaving Joanie money for college. Joan went to college in Hawaii and became a teacher.

Helen moved to New York and ran an agency for employing women.

Remet Heald and remarried him. Divorced him when she discovered he had Parkinson's

Disease. (Heald had strip mines in Pennsylvania)

Uncle Louie (the kleptomaniac) made fun of Bobby when she went to find a job in America because she couldn't speak English. She came home with a job and stuck her tongue out at uncle Louie! (Bobby was a trained weaver. She wove the finest worsted wool for mens' suits). When mom was driving with aunt Josephine and uncle Fred Konrad in their touring car they saw a gazing ball in someone's garden. Aunt Josephine said "uncle Louie better not see that"

After school mom's girlfriend walked home with her specifically to tattle on her! Grandma Chalabala opened the door and the girl began to tattle. Grandma Chalabala leaned forward, grabbed mom and pulled her into the house and said "You're no better!" and slammed the door. Mom thought two things: 1. she wasn't angry; and 2. grandma liked her! (No one in Europe ever said they loved her. It wasn't done).

Grandpa Chalabala's house was only one house away from the train tracks in Brno. Mom could hear the train's whistle as she fell asleep. So to this day she loves train whistles.

(She spent afternoon after school at grandma Smejkal's house and evenings at Chalabala's house with Bobby)

Smejkal means a man tipping his hat and bowing.

Mom came home on Friday to make noodle dough: one egg, flour and salt.

Mom rolled it out on the kitchen table. Bobby would "wash" it with a dusting of flour. She'd roll the dough up and then slice it into tiny "wedding" noodle, regular noodles and flakes. Bobby laid it all out on a white sheet in the basement room to dry.

Recipes and Memoirs from a Czech-American Kitchen

Dec 6 the day when St. Nicholas and the devil came to the house.

St. Nicholas' day – grandpa and brother in tub; mom in the john at school and the devil (chain dragging) and St. Nicholas came in; Bobbi would not let them in her house to scare mom. Cookie on sill if you're good and a piece of coal on the sill if you're naughty.

One of Bobbi's brothers (a step brother) got a lump of coal and never got over it. He went into the army (17 to 20 years) and was killed. Bobby felt so sorry for him.

Christmas eve- no gifts exchanged; that was done on St. Nicholas' day, December 6- mom tried to stay awake to see Baby Jesus arrive. Fish (carpe) served because of the bone in its head shaped like a cross.

Christmas day- got to see the tree ablaze with real candles held on by clips (never a fire). Cookies decorated and hung on tree no ornaments. Knelt in front of the crèche and said Our Father and Hail Mary.

Red ball about the size of a grapefruit.(6 years old)

Doll and pram almost moms' size(7 years old). Beautiful china head and so forth, as tall as she was. She didn't play with it because it was so lovely. Mom had it leaning against the door and someone opened the door and it fell over and the head broke. Mom was so shocked that it had happened that she went into a trance; Bobbi had to slap her face to bring her out of it. Grandpa sent away to Germany for another head. It cost 2 weeks wages. Mom never touched the doll again.

Josephine, mom's dead sister was named after grandpa's mother. Died at 6 months. When they came to America, Bobbi went to the baby's grave the only time, to say good-bye.

Mom used to buy live carp at the city market here in Indianapolis and take it to Bobbi who would let it swim in a washtub to clean itself out before cooking it.